Drui
CLAIMING
SUPERNATURAL BONDS

Jory Strong

ELLORA'S CAVE
ROMANTICA® PUBLISHING

What the critics are saying...

ॐ

5 Stars "Jory Strong brings the reader the fourth story in the *Supernatural Bonds* series. [...] Add magic, supernatural alliances and misunderstandings to the mix and the story has plot twists that will keep the reader glued to the pages of this book. The story is exciting and extremely hot. Make sure the cold shower works before beginning this book! ~ *Sensual EcataRomances Reviews*

"Dragons, Sjen, and Drui! Jory Strong's creative powers know no bounds! I loved her exploration of the supernatural world, of the bonds and magic that exists between different supernatural creatures and even between different worlds. Gently intertwined in that magic is a powerful and full-bodied love story that anyone will enjoy, whether they are quite up on all their supernatural beings or not. [...] Jory Strong keeps the romance hot, the dialogue sizzling, and the action tense. Definitely a winning story." ~ *Romance Junkies Reviews*

An Ellora's Cave Romantica Publication

www.ellorascave.com

Drui Claiming

ISBN 9781419957956
ALL RIGHTS RESERVED.
Drui Claiming Copyright © 2008 Jory Strong
Edited by Sue-Ellen Gower.
Cover art by Syneca.

This book printed in the U.S.A. by Jasmine-Jade Enterprises, LLC.

Electronic book Publication April 2008
Trade paperback Publication August 2008

DRUI CLAIMING

Supernatural Bonds

∾

Trademarks Acknowledgement

Chapter One

ဢ

Dragons! Marika thought. They are TROUBLE. In all caps. They huff and they puff and they burn the house down when they don't get their own way. They're possessive, dominating, and they don't know the meaning of *carefree* because they're weighed down by all the treasure they feel compelled to guard.

So why did she have it so bad for a certain silver-blond male named Xanthus whose dark, dark eyes had a lethal effect on her libido? Why had she continued to play with fire, to go out with him — though she insisted on meeting him at the site of their date and returning home alone afterward — when she knew it was only going to end one way? Badly.

Dragons! This time she picked up one of the pillows on her bed and threw it at the wall in frustration. It struck with a soft thud and dropped to the floor to rest next to an oak seedling in a rune-inscribed ceramic pot.

She refused to keep doing this to herself. The next time she saw Xanthus she was going to tell him she couldn't see him anymore. She'd started to before leaving him at the restaurant earlier, but —

A shiver of erotic fear slid through her as she remembered his expression when she'd once again failed to invite him home with her. It was possessive, dominant, filled with ruthless resolve.

She wasn't delusional enough to convince herself Xanthus would walk away — especially if she came right out and told him there was another man in her life. Competition only made the acquisition of treasure *better* for a dragon.

A low moan escaped as she imagined what telling him about Tallis would mean. It was easy to picture Xanthus sexually feral, putting her on her hands and knees and fucking her in front of a rival male.

Marika unbuttoned her shirt and tossed it aside, then unclasped her bra and did the same. She couldn't stand the confinement any longer. Her breasts were swollen and achy, her cunt lips flushed and slick with need.

She took her nipples between her fingers. Squeezed and tugged. Imagined Xanthus and Tallis suckling her at the same time, their bodies holding her to the mattress, their hard cocks pressed against her thighs while their fingers played in her wet slit.

With a whimper her hands left her breasts to slide underneath the waistband of her skirt and panties. Her fingers went to her stiffened clit. Exquisite sensation spiked through her as she stroked herself, seeking comfort and relief, an escape from indecision and worry.

What was she going to do? She loved Florida.

She loved working for Aislinn Windbourne Dilessio, the half-elf owner of Inner Magick. She treasured their deepening friendship and was close to revealing her own connection to the supernatural world. And there was her blossoming friendship with Detective Storm O'Malley, who Marika thought might have finally figured out—or been told—her new "husbands" were faeries—of the Sidhe kind and not the gay kind. And her friendship with Aislinn's best friend, Sophie, who didn't yet know she was about to become a dragon's mate.

It was as close as Marika had come in a long time to feeling as if she was at home, surrounded by people who actually *saw* the supernatural world, or at least what was left of it after the elves, dragons and most of the fey fled to their own realms. It tore her up to think about leaving Florida, not now, when she was settling in, the wanderlust she'd experienced for most of her life fading away as it did for her kind.

And that was the trouble with falling in a big way for Xanthus. If he knew she was Drui and she could see him for what he was, then he wouldn't hesitate to take her as his mate. Perhaps he'd even return to the dragon realm with her, imprisoning her there as dragons had a reputation of doing with any of the Drui they discovered — well, those they didn't kill outright, though in all honesty, as far as Marika knew, the desire by humans and supernaturals to slaughter her kind belonged in the ancient past.

The Drui started out as a nomadic people who traveled with human tribes known as the Galatai or later, druids, though the humans who called themselves Druid didn't realize true Drui ability came by birthright as well as learning. Her kind were valued for their ability to draw poison and disease from human bodies, and though supernatural beings were rarely afflicted by such things, the Drui could also use their abilities to restore them to health.

They'd been viewed as great healers before the dawn of religions and priests who felt threatened by their abilities, labeling them evil and urging those in power to round them up and kill them. And perhaps because the Drui were in a fight for survival, some of them used their ability to heal supernaturals, not to draw away poison and disease but to draw power — the magical lifeblood — of those beings who weren't human.

As soon as the supernaturals realized what the Drui were capable of, they began hunting them as well. Enslaving some, killing others, and mating with a few in the hope of gaining control over such a powerful ability, until finally those who remained alive and free went into hiding, remaining so even after the strongest of the supernaturals fled this world for realms they created from their own magic.

Marika shivered. She didn't fear Xanthus would hurt her. Being Drui would make her a greater prize to him, especially given the wizard's curse tying dragon fertility to the Chalice of Enos.

11

She knew Xanthus would protect and guard her. She thought he might even be willing to remain in this realm, but despite wanting Xanthus with a desperation bordering on painful, she couldn't risk letting him claim her as his mate. Dragons didn't share and she came from a long line of tree-hugging, multi-partnered Drui.

There were threesomes, foursomes, fivesomes. Her great uncle and his brother shared four wives, and enjoyed it immensely when their wives went at it with one another!

There were *no* twosomes. And while the thought of seven husbands, one for each day of the week, was an amusing fantasy, Marika had always known that when push came to shove and the need to "settle and nest" overwhelmed her, she'd take two husbands.

If the two men in her life and bed wanted to do each other, she was all for it. But one of those men was already a given.

As if on cue, a sleek, golden cat slid through the opening between door and jamb. His collar gleamed with rune-etched gems as he prowled across the room. With lithe grace he jumped up on the bed, morphing into a panther-size version of himself before becoming human in appearance, honey-blond with eyes as dark as hers, the jeweled collar braided from the black strands of her hair still around his neck.

He purred, lips parting slightly to inhale and taste the scent of her arousal. His eyes glinted. "You smell of dragon and mistress and heat. You need me, but I don't intend to play the part of dragon lover or allow you to confuse me for him."

"Tallis," Marika said, her body growing heavier with need. She might have saved his life years ago and accidentally enslaved him in the process, but he was the sexual master in their relationship.

A moan escaped when Tallis reached over, jerking her skirt and panties down to reveal arousal-slick fingers caressing an erect clit.

"He did this to you?" Tallis asked, his voice a menacing purr though Marika knew he looked forward to the day she brought another male home to share their bed.

"Yes," she answered.

Tallis leaned down, laved her fingers with a cat-rough tongue and made her cunt clench. Arousal gushed from her slit at his nearness to her needy clit and parted cunt lips.

"He's wrong for us," Tallis said. "He's dangerous. Find a shapeshifter who calls this world home, or take one of the fey who don't claim allegiance to the Sidhe as a mate."

Marika started to pull her hand away from her swollen folds. Tallis' hiss stopped her.

"I already decided to tell him I wouldn't see him again," she said, canting her hips, begging silently for Tallis' caress.

Tallis rubbed his tongue over the backs of her fingers and hand, sent heated breath over fevered flesh. "Finish it."

A shudder went through her. Sometimes she fought him, but this time she didn't have the will to, not when she ached so badly and knew he'd reward her with even greater pleasure if she yielded.

Marika pressed her fingers into her slit. Coated them with arousal before returning to her clit, stroking the underside before swirling over the tiny naked head.

Icy shards of sensation shot through her, curling her toes and making her hips jerk upward. Liquid heat slid downward, over the rosette of her anus.

Marika panted. Imagined what it would be like to have both Tallis and Xanthus inside her at the same time, their cocks rubbing against each other as they fucked her.

Need defined her, a savage emptiness that felt soul deep. She rubbed and stroked her clit, desperate to come so Tallis would touch her.

Her eyes never wavered from his as she watched the hunger build in him, as she thrilled at the way his nostrils flared and his purr deepened. She whimpered when Tallis rose to his knees, positioned himself between her thighs, his thick cock hard against his abdomen, the heavy globes of his testicles hanging beneath it in a display of masculinity.

"Say his name when you come," Tallis ordered and her breathing grew ragged, her movements rough, nearly violent until finally the hot fury of lust broke over her and she cried out Xanthus' name.

"Better?" Tallis purred.

"Yes," Marika said, though she knew the languid satisfaction wouldn't last for long.

"Good. Now there won't be any confusion about who's attending to your needs."

"As if I could ever confuse anyone else for you."

Firm masculine fingers clamped around her wrists. She shivered when he took her hands to his mouth, cleaned the evidence of her orgasm away with his cat-rough tongue.

"Tallis," she whispered, trembling in anticipation of having him lean down and do the same to her pussy.

"I should make you wait," Tallis said, but he knew he wouldn't. Her warm scent and honeyed wetness were driving him crazy. The sight of her splayed thighs and parted, dusky slit had him only a few thrusts away from coming.

Still, he didn't immediately do her bidding. She needed to be reminded that the choice of a second mate wasn't hers alone. She needed to be reminded that his fate and hers were intertwined, and he knew best how to keep both her heart and her body safe.

A dragon was out of the question. In his long lifetime he'd never heard of one sharing a mate. They were notorious for hoarding their treasure. Marika would be a prize on par with the Chalice of Enos that the dragons and fey were frantically searching for.

It was good she'd decided on her own to stop seeing Xanthus, though Tallis well understood why she was drawn to the dragon. Xanthus might not be powerful enough to remain in this realm unless tied in liege service to Severn Damek, but he was still a heady mix of dominant masculinity.

A shudder went through Tallis as Xanthus' image came to mind. He'd seen him from afar—and closer, through cat eyes. It was all too easy to imagine him and Xanthus wrestling, testing their strength against one another, fighting to see which one would mount Marika first.

It was the way of his kind, the Sjen, to protect, to ensure fertility—and to grow more powerful when those they guarded took mates and had children. He'd thought the wanderlust of a young Drui would never leave Marika, but finally, finally she was settling, and he would ensure she took the right mate—for both of them.

Tallis cupped his testicles, weighing and fondling them as the fingers of his other hand encircled his cock, measuring it with a stroke upward, remeasuring it with a stroke downward.

Marika's breath caught. Her scent intensified as she watched him touching himself. Her hands went to her breasts, delicate fingers finding dark nipples and making fire streak through his penis.

"Don't," Tallis growled, knowing she'd soon be arching her back, pleading with him to suck her and the power between them would shift. He'd be helpless against her.

Tallis freed his cock and testicles in favor of pinning her open thighs to the mattress. He leaned down, rubbed his cheek over her bare mound and tiny clit.

He loved her smoothness, her heat, the softness of her skin and the way she was always wet for him. Hers was the smell and taste, the feel of home. It had been so from the very first.

"Please," she whimpered and he lashed her with his tongue, its cat-rough texture adding to her pleasure, making her hips lift from the mattress and her cunt lips grow more swollen.

Honeyed arousal slid from her opening. He lapped it up, piercing her with just the tip of his tongue before stroking over her clit.

It was paradise. She was a paradise he never got enough of.

Not a day passed when he didn't claim her with his cock. Not an hour passed when he didn't think about her.

From the very first Marika had been his world, his focus. He had never resented the accidental bond forged between them when she'd saved his life.

At the time she'd thought she was saving an alley cat. Instead she'd bound herself to a Sjen.

Usually his kind presided over a house or place, but from the very moment he'd felt her touch and looked through her eyes to her soul, he'd presided over her, moving from place to place as the wanderlust of the Drui young ordained.

He could share her with other males. For his kind it heightened the passion and strengthened them. But he was glad she wanted only two men in their bed. Now he would see to the task of ensuring the second one was suitable.

A soft rumbling purr escaped as she whimpered, begged prettily for him to fuck her with his tongue. Tallis thrust into her, felt molten lust surge through his cock in waves as her inner muscles clamped down on him, held his tongue inside her.

She moaned when his tongue retreated. He rewarded her needy sounds with a swirling assault on her tiny clit, with hard sucks that had her keening, hips lifting off the bed.

Every sound fed his hunger, filled his soul with the symphony of passion, reinforced the bond between them. He turned his head slightly, bit her inner thigh, then licked over the spot.

Thoughts of Xanthus, images of him mounting her, taking her with a dragon's cock and making her scream in ecstasy, intruded. Tallis bit Marika again, washed over the place with his tongue before laving the swollen folds of her labia and her rigid clit.

She thrashed underneath him, liquid heat sliding from her channel, coating the perfect rosette of her back entrance before wetting the sheets. He growled when he saw she'd forgotten his earlier command, or ignored it.

Delicate fingers gripped alluring dark areolas, pinched and twisted, pulled—giving pleasure that didn't come from him, pleasure he hadn't granted. He rose to his knees again, reveled in the way she cried at the loss of his presence between her thighs, at the way her lashes fluttered open and her eyes flashed with erotic fear in the instant before he delivered a sharp, light slap to her bare pussy and hardened clit.

Her hips jerked upward but her hands remained on her breasts, her fingers tight on the dark nipples that were his to suck, his to pleasure. Tallis spanked her again, harder this time.

"You know better," he said, watching her struggle against twin desires—whether to yield so he'd fuck her soon or to fight and drive the passion higher.

She knew he could torment her for hours, could keep her on the edge of orgasm until she was crying, quivering with the need to have him inside her, filling her with his cock and letting her come. Tallis slapped her mound again, then covered it with his hand, trapping the heat of his discipline against her bare flesh and pressing his palm to the naked head of her clit.

He saw Marika's surrender in her eyes, knew utter satisfaction when her hands fell away from her breasts. "Don't make me wait any longer, Tallis. I need you."

The words stroked his soul, sent icy-hot spikes of desire pulsing through his cock. He rubbed her bare cunt, petting her to let her know she'd pleased him.

She whimpered when he stopped touching her, but hastened to obey when he said, "Get on your elbows and knees."

Raw, primal hunger filled Tallis at the sight of her offering herself to him—dusky buttocks in the air, her thighs spread to reveal her swollen cunt lips and wet slit. He leaned in, lapped at her heated flesh until she was shaking, moaning, her scent deepening, becoming an intoxicating lure and announcing she was ready to take permanent mates.

A shudder went through him along with the sudden unwelcome thought that somehow the dragon's potent pheromones were responsible for the more rapid change in her. Before meeting Xanthus, she'd slowly been settling, subconsciously choosing this area as her home, her territory, but now Marika's scent told him it *was* her home.

Tallis growled, not wanting to think about the dragon. He covered her with his body and thrust into her aggressively, groaned when she clamped down on him mercilessly.

White heat scorched him. Burned through his cock and filled his veins with fiery lust. His heart beat with it. His soul was consumed by it.

When she'd saved his life while he was in the cat's form, she'd changed him, blended a human shape with that of a feline, giving him retractable claws and backward facing spines on his penis.

He panted with each stroke, silently chanted her name. Her tight sheath made him work at pleasing her, made him fight against letting the spines descend to rake across her inner muscles and make them both scream with ecstasy as his semen poured into her.

Her cries filled the room. Her scent grew more intoxicating. The sound of flesh striking flesh drove him to pound into her harder, faster. She was his world, his only reality, his paradise as well as his mate.

Sharp claws pierced the bedding, gripped the mattress as Marika lowered her torso, pressing her breasts to the sheet, rubbing her nipples against the fabric, changing the angle so he went deeper, got so close to her womb that the last of his control burned away. White fire raced down his spine in a hot warning that had him growling, pistoning faster, finally letting the spines on his cock descend to make them both come.

Shudder after shudder racked him as he filled her with his seed, as her channel clamped down on him hungrily, milking him of everything he possessed and leaving him lightheaded. He sheathed his claws and collapsed with her in his arms, his penis still inside.

The sounds of heavy breathing gave way to a contented rumbling purr. He nuzzled Marika, rubbed his cheek against hers and smiled as she mumbled sleepily.

His thoughts returned to Xanthus and some of his contentment dissipated. Dragon's pheromones were potent. It was possible Marika was reacting to Xanthus as any mostly human female might, but it was also possible her body had chosen the dragon as a mate.

The thought of it had Tallis pulling her more tightly against him, hardening inside her, the spines on his cock descending just enough to lock it into position. For a fleeting second he considered taking her to South America, to the lair of a jaguar shapeshifter who would make an excellent second, or perhaps to Scotland where it might be possible to form a union with a fey cat-sith.

The dragons were consumed with their quest for the Chalice of Enos and Xanthus was bound by his liege service to Severn Damek. There'd be no chance of him following, and should the dragons find their precious cup and restore their fertility, freeing Xanthus to come after Marika, it would be too late by then.

With another mate to guard Marika, along with the limits she'd already set on her heart—to bond with only two men— Xanthus wouldn't easily be able claim her and take her to the dragon's realm. He was at a disadvantage in this magic-poor place and less powerful than he would be in world the dragons now claimed, a parallel universe accessible only through guarded portals.

Marika whimpered, a confused, pained sound. And as if she guessed the direction of his thoughts, she whispered, "Xanthus," calling another male's name while Tallis' cock was still lodged inside her.

Tallis' lips pulled back. A low growl replaced the purr. Instinct and genetic programming clashed with logic.

The Sjen need to take care of Marika won out. The duty to guard her expanding, requiring him to learn more about Xanthus.

Tallis cupped her breast, rubbed his palm over her nipple. He moaned when her sheath clamped down on him.

There was no choice. Tomorrow he would go where the dragons were sure to gather like sharks — to the auction being held at the VanDenbergh estate — the place where a man had been murdered and the Dragon's Cup stolen.

Chapter Two

ஐ

Xanthus closed his eyes as hot water cascaded over him, washing away lathered soap but failing to dissolve the agony holding him in its grip. Embarrassed heat burned his face as memories of waking in twisted, semen-wet sheets returned with a vengeance.

Marika. Even her name had the power to drive him to his knees, to make him fight to stay in human form.

His fingers captured his penis in a fist, stroking upward as his other hand went to his heavy sac. With a growl he let some of the magic fade away to reveal a cock engorged past what any human male was capable of.

Xanthus shuddered as his fist glided over the twin rings of thick cartilage circling beneath the head of his penis. Their sole purpose was to stimulate the female of his species into ovulating, but he had no intention of taking a dragon for a mate. He wanted Marika.

The growl deepened. Frustration, desire, the need to claim her without the freedom to do so, all of it weighed down on him, left him feeling raw and savage—dangerous.

It'd been that way since Trace Dilessio, a human cop he owed a favor to, had called in that favor. Trace wanted his wife, Aislinn, the half-elf who owned Inner Magick, guarded.

The task was easy enough—until Marika stepped through the doorway of Trace's house and into Xanthus' life. He'd pursued her since then, tried to court her as a human male might—and failed despite the way her scent and sultry glances told him she wanted him as desperately as he wanted her.

So far Marika had avoided being alone with him in any place where he could mount her and claim her as his mate. It was almost as if she knew he wasn't what he appeared to be, guessed somehow he was a dragon.

Xanthus shook his head, causing the long strands of wet white-blond hair to slide over his chest and back. Aislinn wouldn't have told Marika. Neither would the detective, Storm, who was bound to the Sidhe princes, Pierce and Tristan. There were ancient covenants governing them all in this realm, laws forbidding revealing the existence of other supernaturals to any mortal other than a mate—and Marika was not yet a mate.

She would be. Every instinct, every fiber of his being insisted she was the right human female for him, his perfect match. And if Severn, to whom he owed his allegiance and liege service to, was successful in recovering the Chalice of Enos and restoring fertility to the dragon race…

A shudder went through Xanthus. His cock pulsed against his hand. There would be offspring with Marika. Dragon offspring. And because she was human, by law their children would belong to him—though he had no intention of ever allowing Marika to part from him.

He lusted for Marika in a way he'd never done any female—human or supernatural. He spent his days plotting ways to claim her and his nights dreaming of her. And once she became his mate—he would share her with one other male.

A pant escaped as Xanthus imagined what it would feel like to be inside her at the same time another male was, to watch as another touched and took her. He craved it though he'd never experienced it, didn't yet know the full nature of his own sexuality.

When he finally had Marika, would he be like his father, sharing a woman with another male? Or would he be like his grandfather, who made love with both the female and male who shared his bed? Neither his father nor his grandfather had known the full truth of their sexuality until they'd claimed a female and shared her with another male.

Xanthus moaned as he contemplated both scenarios. Sharing was an aberration among dragons. Treasure, hoarding it and guarding it, was everything to them. But then he wasn't purely dragon. Fey blood ran in his veins. And the fey often cared little which sex their lovers were.

He couldn't yet envision the male he would share Marika with. Each time he tried, irritation rippled along his spine, as though the choice wasn't his to make. But every day the need to enter into a bond with Marika and another male grew.

There were moments when desperation seized him and the feeling time was running out sent panic racing through him. He had to mate with her. He had to claim her before duty to Severn was replaced by duty to his family and the quest to be named Kirill's heir.

Xanthus' buttocks clenched as his hand slid up and down his shaft. He let himself fall into the fantasy that his fist was Marika's sheath gripping his penis, that the heated water of the shower was slick arousal, feminine desire.

His hips jerked and his testicles pulled tight against his body. His breathing grew harsh, ragged.

Icy-hot flashes of ecstasy surged through him with each stroke. He tightened his grip to the point where pain and pleasure were a perfect blend, the way it would be when he and another male took Marika at the same time.

The imagery made him thrust faster and harder. Until finally white noise filled his mind and orgasm took him in a violent release of semen.

Xanthus slumped against the wall of the shower stall. The water washed his seed away along with his relief.

Tension filled him, as did his sense of duty and honor. He owed liege service to Severn Damek, one that required him to put aside his pursuit of Marika, at least for those hours of his day belonging to Severn.

Yesterday's arrival of Severn's mother and Audriss, the female who hoped to be Severn's mate, couldn't have come at a worse time—though it wasn't entirely unexpected. The Chalice of Enos had surfaced again after centuries of being well-hidden and Severn had claimed a human mate, one who needed only to be taken to the dragon's realm to have the magic of their bond sealed so they would have a psychic connection.

With a grunt Xanthus pushed himself away from the wall and finished his shower. He made quick work of drying his hair and dressing.

Rather than go to the main kitchen of Severn's estate, where a cook was on duty, Xanthus ate breakfast in the living quarters allotted to him then left to listen to the reports of those working during the night, before finally seeking out Severn. He found Severn in a private dining alcove. As he approached he heard Sophie's panicked whisper. "Someone's coming," followed by Severn's rely. "And they will not dare to look at you, Sophie. Everyone in this household knows you belong to me."

Tension flashed to nearly unbearable heat in Xanthus. He could easily imagine the dominance games Severn would play. Had fantasized playing those same games with Marika.

Xanthus steeled himself not to look at Sophie as he stopped next to the table where they were eating breakfast. His sense of humor asserted itself, silently pointing out that it wasn't fear of Severn that kept him from stealing a glance at the beautiful, well-endowed redhead, but the knowledge a friendship was developing between Sophie and Marika.

"Your mother is not the only one to arrive," Xanthus told Severn. Like the appearance of Severn's mother, news that other ancients had left the dragon realm for this one wasn't surprising given the importance of the Chalice of Enos.

"Who else is here?" Severn asked.

"Malik's ancestor is here, as is Hakon's."

"Where are they?"

"At Drake's Lair." Xanthus' couldn't suppress a small smile. "Malik and Hakon maneuvered their elders to the club. Tielo had the foresight to call Pierce and tell him there were wealthy marks waiting to be relieved of some of their treasure. I believe the old ones have been introduced to the game of Texas hold 'em."

"And my mother?"

"She has not yet left her chambers."

"Audriss?"

A shudder passed through Xanthus. Audriss was not a female he'd wish to be mated to. "She demanded one of your cars and took along a servant to drive her."

"The GPS unit in the car has been enabled?"

"Of course."

"Then I'll leave it to you to monitor her movements. She has spent little time here. I doubt she will consider the advances in technology or guess how thoroughly I've embraced them."

Xanthus nodded and turned, the unintentional glimpse of Sophie's parted blouse making the hunger for Marika return with savage intensity.

* * * * *

Warm sea air and the sound of gulls, they'd come to mean home, Marika thought as she walked to Inner Magick. It was strange how the urge to settle in one place had crept up on her and managed to pounce. It was expected, because eventually it happened to every Drui, but somehow it was still unexpected *to her.*

When she'd come to Florida, she's been so sure it was only temporary. Sun, surf and lovemaking on the beach with Tallis, those were what had brought her. But her reason for staying changed and she could easily trace the feeling of permanency back to the instant when leaving Florida made a knot form in her chest.

It was right after Aislinn was attacked because of a high profile case her uber-macho and totally gorgeous husband, Detective Trace Dilessio, was working on. It was the day she'd gone to Aislinn's home and found Xanthus there.

Marika shivered thinking about him. She felt her body tighten with need and her palms grow damp.

Today was the day she'd stop playing with fire, literally. True, even among her own kind she'd always been a bit of a daredevil and had traveled more extensively than most. But she wasn't foolish enough to venture into the territory of self-delusion and denial.

Dragons hoarded and guarded. It's what they did.

They didn't share their mates or their treasures. They were hardwired not to—which meant despite craving Xanthus like he was some kind of drug designed specifically for her, she had to tell him she wasn't going out with him anymore. Period. End of story.

She couldn't risk ending up in the dragon realm. His thinking she was human might delay the trip for a little while, but eventually he'd learn she was Drui and then—

Another shiver cut through Marika, this one made up of fear. She didn't know what would happen to Tallis if she was taken to the dragon world. Neither of them did. When she'd saved his life, she'd bound him to her in way that shouldn't have happened—even if she knew *why* it had happened.

Marika's fingers caressed the locket at her throat, a tiny heart containing the oak seeds necessary for performing Drui-healings. She'd panicked when the ordinary poisoned cat she thought she was helping turned out to be a spirit entity under attack from black magic and a demon calling. In mid-chant she'd switched to a different incantation, failed to form a transition first, then repeated the error not once, but twice more as the demon energy mutated, trying to escape her pull by burying deeper in the cat's form.

She could easily have died. But she didn't. And neither did Tallis.

For the first year they'd been together, the furthest Tallis could be from her was the other side of a closed bathroom door. Every year since then had increased the distance, but different realms...

She shook her head to clear her thoughts. Resolve firmed her spine and she balled her hands into fists. Today was the day. If she didn't see Xanthus, then she'd call him and tell him over the phone.

Marika rounded the corner and saw Inner Magick, or more accurately, the dragon loitering nearby, looking like a human tourist to the majority of those who noticed him, but not to her. There was no mistaking a dragon's signature energy, it spiked around them in hues of red and orange regardless of what color their scales were in their other form.

Seeing the dragon made her thoughts flash back to the previous day, when Xanthus came to Inner Magick—not to see her—but to ask about Sophie and find out where she lived. While he was there, Sophie had called looking for Aislinn. Intuition or maybe premonition, Marika couldn't shake the feeling that Sophie was Severn Damek's mate.

Marika hurried forward, anxious to get into the shop and talk to Aislinn, wondering if Sophie was inside and the dragon outside there to guard her—which would actually mean Severn was more enlightened than she would have expected— or if the dragon's presence meant Sophie was giving Severn a run for his money.

The image of the dragon prince brought to his knees made Marika smile. She pushed through the front door and found Aislinn putting the new rune sets into a display case.

"Did Sophie talk to you yesterday?" Marika asked, kneeling next to Aislinn.

Aislinn's laugh was answer enough. "Yes. She came to the house. Severn Damek was right behind her."

"They're together?"

"Yes."

"The heartstone recognized Severn?" Marika asked, remembering the necklace Aislinn made for Sophie.

The day she'd seen it on Sophie and learned Aislinn created it was the day Marika had known for sure Aislinn was half-elf. Only the elves could work the stone that reacted when a person was in the presence of their perfect match, and though Aislinn's aura had *seemed* Elven — sometimes, it was close enough to the signature energy of a human sensitive to magic to be confusing.

"Yes the necklace recognized him, though Severn's reaction to Sophie was telling enough." Aislinn's soft laugh was completely infectious.

For a split second Marika was tempted to confide in Aislinn about Tallis and Xanthus. She trusted Aislinn, viewed her as more than a friend, but…

Marika couldn't bring herself to do it, not yet anyway, not when there were suddenly so many supernatural beings in the area, fey and dragon alike, all looking for the Chalice of Enos, and all ruthlessly determined to get it. The rules drilled into her in childhood, the necessity for remaining unseen, unnoticed by the beings who'd left this realm for their own, were too deeply ingrained. After the Dragon's Cup was claimed and things went back to normal, after she found her second mate — *husband* — and knew this was truly the place she'd call home, the territory where she'd align herself with a witch practicing the healing arts, then she'd reveal herself to Aislinn and Sophie and Storm.

A lump formed in Marika's throat as she realized that if necessary, her friendship with Sophie would enable her to ask Severn to order Xanthus to stay away from her if Xanthus wouldn't do it willingly. The thought made a hard, cold knot form in her chest and she tried to lose herself in work to escape it.

* * * * *

Dragons! Tallis thought, basking in heat and potent pheromones. He'd forgotten what a rush being around them could be, especially when testosterone pumped through their veins as it was doing now in the presence of so much treasure and so many other male dragons.

It took incredible effort to suppress the rumbling purr that had become so much a part of him since Marika saved his life. There was no chance of hiding the hardness of his cock. It pressed against the front of his jeans aggressively, in challenge and promise.

Too bad. Neither challenge nor promise would be answered. Not here. And not by a dragon.

Just as he'd never known a dragon to share his mate, he'd also never known a dragon be as flexible as he was when it came to sexuality. Too bad. Seeing Marika mated to a dragon would have been advantageous. He could see that now, surrounded by them. Even the relatively young dragons flocking to this world were still creatures imbued with ancient magic. Sharing Marika with one of them would have fed power into the bond he had with her and given him greater freedom — not that he'd ever be too far from her.

Tallis touched the braided collar around his neck. Marika had crafted it for him as soon as they'd realized what her saving his life had meant for both of them. The collar hid his true nature from other supernaturals, unless he wanted to reveal himself — or she wanted it.

That, too, was the price of being bound so tightly to her. Her wishes could become his command.

Images of Marika as she'd been the night before filled his mind. Lust pooled in his testicles, surged through his penis in icy-hot flashes as he saw her on her knees and elbows, her thighs parted and her vulva slick and swollen. Ready for him. Submissive to him.

A shudder went through Tallis, forcing him to close his eyes for an instant in an effort to regain control of himself. He wanted to blame the fine sheen of sweat coating his skin on dragon heat, longed to attribute the powerful desire to mate on dragon pheromones. But he knew it was more than that. He was reacting so strongly in the presence of dragons because of Marika's desire for Xanthus, because of how much her body wanted the dragon as her second lover.

The knowledge served to remind Tallis of his purpose in coming to the VanDenbergh estate. He needed to learn more about Xanthus, hoped to meet him in a place where they both had to pretend they were fully human.

Tallis moved deeper into the crowded rooms. The auction had drawn a diverse crowd, both human and dragon, but Xanthus wasn't there, despite the presence of Severn Damek and Sophie.

Even at a distance Severn's scent marked her as his mate. His body language screamed possessiveness.

Tallis glided closer to where Sophie stood with Severn and the dragon princes, Hakon and Malik. He'd yet to meet Sophie in his human form, but he knew Marika was becoming increasingly fond of her and viewed Sophie as a friend.

Perhaps that friendship would be advantageous in keeping Marika from ending up in the dragon's realm, Tallis thought. Severn had a reputation for being ruthless, for requiring obedience and loyalty in those who owed him liege service. He'd also carved out an empire in *this* realm. If Severn offered Marika protection before Xanthus could claim her as a mate...

Tallis pondered the possibility of approaching Severn about an alliance. He tried to weigh the risk of Marika revealing her Drui heritage against what he knew of dragon laws and loyalties, but couldn't be certain of the best course of action. Caution won out, followed by the need to leave the auction when Severn made a phone call directing Xanthus, in carefully selected words, to come to the estate and take over the duty of seeing to Sophie's safety.

In all likelihood, Sophie would go to Inner Magick and Marika was there. Tallis didn't intend to be too far away from Marika when Xanthus arrived.

* * * * *

Xanthus. Marika's heart tripped into an unsteady beat as he entered Inner Magick with Sophie. Beyond them, through the glass front of the shop, was Tallis in cat form, his visual presence a reminder of what she had to do.

Marika braced herself as Xanthus came directly toward her. Their eyes met, his burning with possessiveness and desire, hers threatening to fill with tears.

The thought of telling him she wouldn't go out with him again made her throat tighten as if to block the words from escaping. But she knew she *had* to speak them.

Memories crowded in—cozy dinners in nice restaurants, sharing popcorn and kissing during movies at the theater, the Saturday they spent at the amusement park. It wasn't only the way he made her burn that drew her to him, it was the way he'd tried to be human, the way he'd treated her like a priceless treasure.

And that was the problem. For all the fun they'd had together, for all the intensity of the lust flaring to life between them whenever they were together, she couldn't belong *only* to him and she couldn't imagine any dragon sharing a mate.

"I can't go out with you again," she said in a low voice, panic rising when his face took on a determined look.

"Why not?"

For an instant she considered telling him she was in love with someone else. But she couldn't bring herself to hurt Xanthus like that, not when having Tallis in her bed didn't exclude taking a second lover.

Guilt clawed at her insides. She should never have gone out with Xanthus to begin with.

She'd thought—no, she *hadn't* thought, she'd only reacted. Even as stories of ancestors dragged off unwillingly to dragon lairs never to be seen again were filling her mind, her body had been on fire, her mouth agreeing to a date.

"It's complicated," she said, forcing a resolve and finality into her tone that hadn't been there before. "I'm sorry if I led you on. But I can't go out with you again."

Emotion writhed in Xanthus, the dragon's baser instinct to take warring with the man's need to honor law and duty. Marika's lips said one thing, but her body, her scent said another. She was his mate and she wanted him as desperately as he wanted her.

For long moments he controlled his breathing, kept the dragon's fire from escaping through his nostrils in a flame of aggravation. *Complicated!* Complicated was having a female who had yet to give him the opportunity to mount and claim her, who forced him to find relief with his own hand and who invaded his dreams so he woke in tangled sheets, calling her name as he came.

His eyes narrowed as she studiously avoided looking at him. He wondered, not for the first time, if she was ultrasensitive to magic and somehow knew he wasn't what he appeared to be—despite his efforts to court her as a human male would.

It wouldn't surprise him. A mortal sensitive to magic would be drawn to this shop and to Aislinn, just as Sophie was.

Movement made him glance away from Marika. Duty coming between them again. Sophie was heading toward the back room of the shop, most likely going to the apartment above it where she'd been staying recently as she worked on one of her manuscripts.

Xanthus left his position against the counter and caught up to Sophie. "Wait," he said, stopping her with a foot on the first stair. "Let me go up first to make sure it's empty."

Sophie's eyes widened. "Why wouldn't it be empty?"

"There's no reason to expect someone is up there but it's my job to check anyway."

"Are you guarding me?"

Surprise slid through Xanthus, restoring some of his usual good humor. He'd envied Severn for so quickly gaining control of his mate when he found her, but apparently even formidable dragon princes had to tread carefully when it came to managing the female who'd captured their hearts.

Xanthus chuckled and shook his head slightly. "Severn didn't tell you?"

"So you *are* guarding me?"

"Severn is a powerful man and you are his mate. He'd be a fool to leave you unprotected. I believe you have researched him thoroughly enough to know that no one considers him a fool."

Sophie groaned in defeat and stepped away from the stairs so he could go into the apartment first. It took only a few minutes to ensure it was free of danger and the door leading to the external stairs was securely locked.

"Don't leave except through the store," Xanthus warned, waiting for a nod indicating her acceptance of his terms before he left the apartment and returned to Marika so they could discuss *complicated*.

Marika busied herself behind the counter as soon as Xanthus stepped into view. Waves of heat swamped her, hardening her nipples so they pressed aggressively against the front of her shirt. Compared to Sophie and her cousin Storm, Marika knew she looked flat-chested, but she felt Xanthus' full attention on her breasts, devouring them with his eyes just as surely as she felt Tallis' smoldering gaze through the front window.

Marika clamped her legs together in reaction, knew even as she did it there was no hiding her arousal from him. Her panties were wet from being in his presence, her clit rigid.

She did her best to ignore Xanthus. The last thing she wanted was for Tallis to feel the need to intervene. It was almost a relief when the door to Inner Magick opened, interrupting the silent battle taking place between Xanthus and her — *almost* because the sleek, beautiful woman who stepped into the shop wasn't human.

Chapter Three

∾

Marika didn't need to witness the tensing of Xanthus' muscles along with his quick glance at the doorway Sophie would come through to know he was back on serious duty as a bodyguard. The woman was fey and powerful, her elements air and water. The telltale white and blue signature swirls radiating from the very human form were impossible for Marika to miss — though she tried hard to pretend otherwise.

She fought against shivering as frigid air touched her skin, didn't even want to acknowledge that much awareness of someone who might well be from Queen Otthilde's court. It was always better to act completely null — a mortal with no sensitivity to magic at all when in the presence of fey, especially powerful fey.

Aislinn went over to the woman and was speaking to her when Sophie entered the room. Surprise flickered through Marika when Sophie immediately made a beeline to the space between counter and wall. She wondered if Sophie sensed the danger the fey represented and instinctively positioned herself behind Xanthus. A quick glance at Sophie's goosefleshed arms was confirmation.

A soft tinkling sound announced the woman's departure. Sophie abandoned her spot behind the counter. "Who was that?"

Instead of answering Sophie directly, Aislinn looked at Xanthus. "She called herself Neryssa. Do you know of her?"

Xanthus gave a small shake of his head. "I haven't seen her before but I'll speak to Severn about her and tell him she came here." He hesitated slightly then glanced briefly at

Sophie before adding, "Tristan and Pierce could tell you who she is. It would probably be wise to speak with them."

Marika shivered. His reference to the Sidhe princes who claimed Sophie's cousin Storm as their shared wife was all the confirmation she needed Neryssa belonged to Queen Otthilde's court.

"Why did she come to Inner Magick?" Sophie asked Aislinn.

"Neryssa said she was curious about what she'd find here."

Sophie rubbed her arms. "Weird."

Xanthus snorted. "Deadly is a better word. Her kind might be beautiful to look upon, but their glamour masks their poison."

"Her kind?" Sophie asked.

Xanthus shrugged. "You and Aislinn are going to the beach?"

"By way of Starbucks," Aislinn said, looping her arm through Sophie's. "Do you want to drive to your favorite spot or walk to the beach from here?"

"We can walk."

Xanthus turned his attention to Marika. Dark eyes bored into hers with predatory intensity. "This isn't finished between us."

She bit her lip to keep from replying. Xanthus moved to the front door and opened it then followed Sophie and Aislinn out of the shop.

Within minutes Tallis was on the other side of the glass, the rune-inscribed crystals in his collar catching the light as he rubbed against the door in the cat's form. Marika let him in.

He'd once told her a Sjen's truest form was an incorporeal one, which made sense given they were considered guardian spirits. But when she'd saved his life, drawn the demon magic from his body and accidentally bound him to her, he'd become corporeal, though limited to the body of a cat or a man with some distinctly feline features.

Marika's cunt clenched as she remembered what if felt like to have him cover her, thrusting inside her repeatedly until only the pleasure-pain rake of the catlike spines on his cock would give her the release she needed. She shivered, wishing Tallis was in his human form so he could ease the ache in her breasts and between her thighs, but he preferred to escort her to and from Inner Magick as a cat, and Aislinn didn't seem to mind having him in the shop.

Aislinn stopped in long enough to say she was gone for the rest of the day. A rush of customers came afterward, keeping Marika busy and distracting her from thoughts of Xanthus and Tallis until finally it was time to set the alarm and lock up for the night.

She glanced around as she walked away from Inner Magick, half expecting to see a dragon sentinel, but instead seeing only lesser fey, their inhuman shapes and malicious expressions the stuff of nightmare. Marika was careful not to allow her attention to linger on them. They thought they were invisible to her and she didn't want them to think otherwise. Their chill reached her along with the sea breeze, telling her they most likely called Otthilde their queen, just as the more powerful Neryssa did.

Usually she walked along the ocean on her way to and from work, sometimes on the beach, sometimes on the boardwalk. The presence of the fey made her uneasy, indecisive. She glanced down at Tallis, who rose onto his hind legs in an uncommon request for her to pick him up.

There was a shortcut home. It would take her through alleyways. Normally it was safe, but... Marika let instinct guide her. She traveled her usual route, going toward the ocean and fighting to prevent any hint of tension from transmitting itself to the fey following her.

They couldn't know she was Drui, couldn't have recognized Tallis as Sjen. So the reason for their presence had to be dragon-related, Xanthus' unmistakable interest in her along with his connection to Severn Damek and the frantic search for the Chalice of Enos.

Marika's arms tightened on Tallis without meaning too, earning her a hiss and the threat of claws. She loosened her grip, knew as soon as they got home he'd demand they leave the area until the business with the Dragon's Cup was settled. He'd argue she needed to have another male in her bed before they returned and tell her he had candidates in mind.

Everything inside her protested against the idea of leaving. She couldn't imagine opening her heart or her body to anyone other than Tallis and Xanthus.

Sharp nails dug into her arm, forcing her attention outward. Fear rippled down her spine at the sight of the fey in front of her. They were whispering into the ear of a drug addict stretched out on a bench, his skeletal form and needle-pocked arms all she needed in order to identify him.

Again Marika acted instinctively. She took the staircase down to the sand. It was hard not to run, not to let her fear give her away. Even if they didn't know she was Drui, the fey were never fond of humans who had *the sight*.

She could guess why they were targeting her. Despite her human blood, Aislinn was still elf. And both Sophie and Storm were guarded by supernatural mates.

Marika's heart hammered in her chest. Out of the corner of her eye she saw the fey scramble to a blanket on the beach where several rough-looking teenage boys were gathered, the area around them littered with beer cans.

She increased her pace when the boys' laughter turned dangerous and suggestive, conscienceless with fey whispers. Her reaction was normal, acceptable, not likely to cause suspicion.

Ahead was the pier, its darkness offering hope as well as the potential for horror. Marika broke out into a run when she heard the boys' footsteps coming after her. Getting to the pier was her only chance of staying safe, not just from the humans chasing her but from the fey who'd whispered malicious thoughts into the boys' minds.

She was gasping by the time she reached the pier, her lungs burning and her sides aching. The choice of how to protect her belonged to Tallis. He could cloak her in shadow, or he could use physical force.

Tallis leapt from her arms as soon as the gloom underneath the pier provided enough cover, became a golden-skinned man clad in black before cat paws could even touch the sand. He was death incarnate, violence personified and even in their drunken state, the teens slid to a halt when they saw him.

Marika prayed they'd back off. She didn't want to see them hurt even though their willingness to come after her was proof of their moral weakness. The lesser fey couldn't command, they could only suggest a course of action.

She sickened when one of the boys stepped forward, his hands spread in supplication, his words horrifying in one so young. "Hey man, we're just looking for a little fun. We got no problem sharing the bitch if you want a piece of her."

Tallis went completely still, a panther in human shape, ready to spring, to go for the kill. Marika's hand shook as she reached out and touched his back, silently willing him not to use deadly force.

"She's mine," Tallis said, his voice little more than a growl.

"I don't think so," the boy said, reaching into his pocket and pulling out a knife. It opened with a snick, revealing a long, sharp blade. "We saw her first."

Another boy, emboldened by the first, pulled out a knife as well. But the third and fourth, less drunk or less depraved, stepped back, distancing themselves from the fight they saw looming.

Tallis didn't wait to attack, didn't waste words. He lunged forward, striking lightning fast, his claws extending and retracting so quickly Marika couldn't see them.

The two boys screamed as they fell to their knees. Blood gushed from their chests and arms.

She stepped forward involuntarily, her hand going unconsciously to the locket containing oak seeds, the Drui desire to heal rushing to the surface. Tallis stopped her, shackled her in a masculine grip. "They'll live," he said, pulling her away, turning his back on the boys with a casualness that spoke of absolute confidence.

* * * * *

Xanthus stopped in front of the door to Severn's private suite. Despite how maddening his own pursuit of a mate was becoming, it gave him pleasure to witness Severn's happiness. It amused him to see how well matched Severn and Sophie were.

Severn was known for his ruthlessness, but also his fairness. For Xanthus, it had been an easy decision to pledge his loyalty to Severn. One he didn't regret, even now, when duty warred with the burning, overpowering urge to claim a mate.

He'd come to this realm hoping for two things. The first was a chance to seek out ancient magic-rich treasure in order to be named Kirill's heir so his fey grandmother would have no trouble accessing the portal leading to the human world. His second reason for living among mortals was to gain a human mate, one who would be as soft and submissive as a female dragon was tough and controlling.

There were males who enjoyed battling with dragon females for supremacy, just as there were males who accepted being dominated, but he wasn't one of them. And beyond that, he was no prize for a female dragon.

He had wealth as it was defined in human terms, valuable gems littered the floor of his private lair and formed a bed. But neither he nor his immediate family was in possession of ancient, pre-exodus treasure, and the territory they held in the dragon realm was rugged and harsh when compared to others. Beyond that, the fey blood in his lineage was abhorrent to most female dragons, as was the knowledge that if he proved to be the same as his grandfather and father, he would share his mate and perhaps himself with another male.

Xanthus knocked on Severn's door. Reporting on the events of the day was his final duty. He suppressed a smile when Severn stepped into the hallway, his reluctance to leave Sophie obvious.

"Shall I summon someone to guard the door?" Xanthus asked.

"The cameras monitoring this hallway are activated?"

"Yes. I assumed you'd want it done before leaving her unattended. If anyone approaches the room, we will be summoned."

"Good."

They went to Severn's office and closed the door.

"What have you learned?" Severn asked.

"Your mother went no further than Drake's Lair. She visited briefly with Malik's and Hakon's ancestors, but those within hearing range say it was not a friendly conversation. They are old rivals."

"And Audriss?"

"Before we speak about her, I talked to both Pierce and Tristan and asked them about the fey who appeared at Inner Magick while Sophie was there. Neryssa is Morgana's cousin. Morgana once had a claim on Tristan. It's one of the reasons he settled in this realm. He had no wish to bed her by order of the queen. When the chalice resurfaced she was sent here and learned of Storm and her importance to Tristan and Pierce. Before they could fully claim Storm as their mate, Morgana attempted to kill her. Tristan and Pierce send an offer to help in any way they can. Morgana is capable of taking vengeance by using Sophie as a surrogate for Storm. Queen Otthilde will look the other way and claim ignorance even as she celebrates the death of a dragon's mate."

Severn nodded. "Neryssa's element is water?"

"More air than water but she can wield and become both."

"Audriss was seen with one of them?"

"Morgana." Xanthus frowned. "It occurred while I was guarding Sophie so I didn't witness it with my own eyes. The one who reported it said it could have been a chance meeting or an arranged one. From outward appearances the exchange appeared to be unfriendly and yet it lasted longer than one would expect."

"Where was it?"

"At the beach. Close to the surf. Morgana walked out of the water as though she'd been swimming. There was no way to hear what was said without revealing to Audriss that she was being followed."

"And afterward?"

"Audriss went by Drake's Lair, which is where I found her with your mother when you claimed Sophie at the police station. From Drake's Lair she came here. Unfortunately I didn't know you and Sophie were on the grounds until it was too late to prevent an encounter with Audriss." Amusement flickered through Xanthus' at the trail of clothing he'd found in the maze, though his enjoyment of it was tempered by the hard state of his cock. "But I gather you were able to salvage the situation."

"Yes, all is well with my mate." Severn's smile held a wealth of masculine satisfaction.

Silence settled between them for a moment. It was broken when Severn said, "You have been spending a lot of time at Inner Magick. Is Marika a passing fancy or a serious interest?"

Xanthus stiffened. It was answer enough. Unspoken between them was the acknowledgement that until the Dragon's Cup was found or the danger presented by those from Queen Otthilde's court was past, Severn wouldn't release him from his duty of guarding Sophie.

The fey held an advantage in this realm. Dragons were prohibited by the ancient covenants from taking their true form while the fey were allowed to be in their elemental states.

In dragon form, Severn or any of those guarding Sophie could see fey essence. In human form they could only sense the presence of fey beings in non-human form when they were very close.

Xanthus was different. Because of his fey blood, he could reliably sense the fey at a greater distance, regardless of whether they wore flesh or hid in their elemental nature.

"If you wish to bring the female here so she can be protected you are welcome to do so," Severn said. "As soon as the chalice is recovered, I will seal the bond with Sophie and then take her away for a while. I will consider that your service to me has been completed until the next tithe period begins. As far as I am concerned, you will be free to stay among the mortals with my protection or return to the dragon realm as you choose."

Xanthus tilted his head in acknowledgement. One corner of his mouth curled in self-directed amusement. "I would love nothing more than to bring Marika here and tie her to my bed. Unfortunately we are engaged in a slight…battle at the moment. She'll be safe enough at Inner Magick. There is no reason to think the fey or dragon females will take an interest in her."

"Assign some of the others to guard her when you can't be there if you feel the need to do so."

Xanthus nodded. The thought of drawing another male dragon's attention to Marika before he'd mated with her made him feel like a fledgling barely able to control his fire.

He trusted those in Severn's service with his life, but dragons were acquisitive and fiercely competitive by nature. In ancient times, before they'd fled this realm, males would steal any human mate left unguarded. The females were a prize beyond value because so few of them survived the shock of being taken away from their families by creatures they saw as terrifying beasts. The ones who did accept a dragon male would — given enough time — usually respond to a new mate.

In those days there was no right or claim to ownership except for possession. Dragon culture had evolved since then. But old instincts, especially surrounding a human mate, remained.

Instinct and logic fought until Severn tipped the scales, shocking Xanthus to his core by saying, "I made an agreement with Hakon and Malik about the fate of the Dragon's Cup. We sealed it in the traditional way, by blood oath. When the chalice is found, either by our joint effort or separate endeavors, it will be taken to Drake's Lair. Any male who wishes to drink from it with his mate will be allowed to do so without discrimination or price while we seek a way to break the spell tying our fertility to the cup."

Xanthus was so stunned he could only nod. Dragons hoarded and guarded. What Severn and the other dragon princes had agreed to was almost unimaginable, and yet — all three princes called this realm home, all three had adapted, gained wealth and power, and more importantly, enough magic to allow other dragons to stay in a place greatly weakened by the creation of separate worlds and the exodus of supernatural beings into them.

Excitement rose inside Xanthus, never had he felt more optimistic about the future and the reclaiming of the Chalice of Enos. He turned away after being dismissed and retrieved the cell phone from his pocket, sent someone to guard Marika.

Xanthus' contentment lasted only until he reached the rooms assigned to him. A frown drew his eyebrows together when his phone rang and he recognized the very number he'd dialed only moments earlier. He answered it, felt fire scorch through him when the dragon calling him said, "She just returned home. There's a human male with her. His body language is possessive and she's accepting of his hands on her. Do you wish me to act?"

Chapter Four

ဢ

Do you wish me to act?

The words and the image of Marika with another male—one he hadn't yet accepted—were a roar across Xanthus' soul. The magic holding him into a human form threatened to burn away and for the second time in one day emotion writhed inside him, the dragon's baser instinct *to take* warring with the man's need to honor law and duty.

Once again he found himself fighting to control his breathing, to keep the dragon's fire from escaping through his nostrils and mouth in a flame of aggravation. *It's complicated,* she'd said, *I can't go out with you again.* But her body and scent told him otherwise.

She was his mate and she wanted him as desperately as he wanted her. It was as simple as that.

He'd wondered about his inability to choose a male to share her with, had even toyed with the idea the choice wasn't his to make. Now he knew the reason for it.

Xanthus exhaled slowly, the trappings of humanity he'd worked so hard to acquire in this realm winning out. He grimaced at the thought of sharing Marika with a human male, someone who was powerless to protect her against a supernatural threat. But if her heart was already held, in part, by a mortal, then he had no choice but to proceed carefully and cautiously. He had no wish for her to hate him. If the human male was the only obstacle in his path to claiming Marika for his mate, then Xanthus felt up to the task.

"Do you wish me to act, Xanthus?"

"Continue with your duties," Xanthus said before closing the cell phone and shedding his clothing, then lying on the bed. He curled his fingers around his cock and tried to imagine the human male Marika had chosen, wondered as he had throughout his life whether he would follow his father's example or his grandfather's when it came to his female's other mate.

* * * * *

"Strip," Tallis said, he eyes narrowing when Marika whirled and crossed her arms beneath her breasts instead of obeying.

"I won't leave." Her stiff posture and taut features screamed her commitment to the stance she'd taken. Her words revealed she'd already guessed at his thoughts, his intention to take her away from the danger the dragons and fey presented as they scrambled to recover the Chalice of Enos.

Tallis' nostrils flared with the press of her will against his. His lips pulled back in a baring of teeth as the collar around his neck tightened and the runes woven into it flared to life.

He wasn't accustomed to her defiance. They rarely battled over what was best for her.

There'd been mock fights, a clash of wills to drive the sexual tension between them higher and to give him reason to punish her, but this was different. And he knew who lay at its root. Xanthus.

"Strip, Marika." This time it was a growled warning, accompanied by the unbuckling of his belt, the slow slide of it through the loops of his pants.

"No," she said, but her body gave a different answer.

Hardened nipples pressed against her shirt. Her chest rose and fell rapidly. She shivered and wet her lips, her gaze riveted to the strip of leather in his hands.

In his mind's eye he saw her draped over his lap, smooth dusky buttocks positioned for the punishment she deserved for defying him. She *knew* he desired only to serve and please her, to keep her safe from any threat of danger.

She was his world. He was bound completely to her, their lives and fates intricately and forever entwined.

The slap of leather against skin, the belt against his palm, heated the air with the scent of arousal — hers as well as his. "If I tell you again, your punishment will be more severe."

Her scent deepened. Rebellion over their future gave way to the lust they shared in the present. The fight inside her shifted, desire for instant gratification pitted against the temptation to draw out the moment when she would submit.

Tallis struck his palm again with the soft belt, widened his stance and had to fight to keep a moan from escaping. The complete trust she had in him was a potent aphrodisiac.

His cock pressed aggressively against the material of his pants, throbbed with desperate urgency to push inside her and be held in heated ecstasy. The tip of his penis was already wet. His testicles heavy and full, promising not just the single release of seed, but repeated ejaculations until he was too weak to move off her, too ensnared to want to.

He opened his mouth to order her to strip again, but before the words could be uttered, her fingers were at the opening of her blouse, slowly freeing the buttons, drawing their play out but not directly defying him.

Another surge of icy-hot lust spiked through his cock. He opened his pants, let her see what she'd done to him, what belonged to her, though *he* would decide when she got it.

Her whimper was music to his ears, a song to soothe the predatory beast she'd turned him into when she melded his spirit to the cat's. He kicked off his shoes and let his pants fall to the ground before stepping out of them. His shirt followed, along with hers.

Marika toyed with the front clasp of her bra, a hesitation that almost had him closing the distance between them and freeing her breasts, worshipping them with his hands and mouth until she screamed in pleasure. It drove him crazy when she doubted her appeal, thought her breasts small when he found them perfect.

He fought the urge to go to her. Knew that if he suckled, he'd soon be inside her, thrusting uncontrollably, helpless against her allure.

Tallis tapped the leather of the belt against his thigh in silent warning. She opened her bra, tormented him by covering pebbled dusky nipples with her hands, a virginal display of shyness she knew made him wild for her.

"Marika." It was a promise of retribution that edged far too close to a plea.

Her quickly hidden smile told him she'd heard it too. She shed the bra, took her own sweet time unzipping her skirt.

It fell to the floor, leaving her in delicate sandals and ultrafeminine panties. Arousal glistened on her inner thighs. Her clit pressed against the front of the sheer fabric, begging for his fingers, his lips, his tongue.

Another tap of the belt against his thigh and she slipped off her shoes. "Where do you want me?" she whispered, her gaze going to the chair, fueling fantasies of bending her over his lap, of pulling down the barely there panties and spanking her as her hot flesh rubbed against his hard cock.

"On the bed," he said, denying them both, fearing the temptation she posed. He couldn't allow her to gain the upper hand, not in this battle or the one to come.

He reminded himself of his purpose in dominating her. He wanted her compliance. *Needed it.*

The fey attack changed things. They had to leave, at least for a little while, lest they become the victims as faerie and dragon both searched for the Chalice of Enos.

"Are you sure you want me on the bed?" Marika asked, sliding the panties over shapely, tanned thighs and letting them drop to form loose, lacy cuffs around her ankles.

Tallis moved into her, knowing it was a mistake even as he did it. He crowded her, nearly went to his knees when her hands settled on his chest in supplication, her palms against tiny, masculine nipples, her dark eyelashes sweeping downward, the picture of submissiveness.

He adored her, loved her beyond measure and reason. Wanted in that instant to be her slave, her servant. But if they were to remain safe, then he needed to be her master.

It took every ounce of self-control he possessed to grip her arm and guide her backward to the bed. When she felt it against the back of her legs, she sat, spared him one last pleading glance.

Tallis shook his head and stepped away from her, felt a primal, soul-deep satisfaction as she rolled to her stomach, presenting her vulnerable buttocks for his inspection and punishment. He smoothed his hand over her tender skin, fought the urge to lean down, to press kisses against the smooth, dusky curve of her ass. If he did it, she'd lift upward, spread her thighs just enough for him to see swollen, parted cunt lips and the dark color of her slit. If that happened, the will to punish her would desert him, replaced by the urge to mate her.

The Drui weren't shapeshifters, but she was feline in so many ways. Sleek and lithe, tiny and feminine, utterly sensuous.

Together or apart, the need to couple with her and fantasies of doing it were always close to the surface of his consciousness. Tallis stroked her buttocks a final time then drew his hand away.

She cried out when the soft leather of the belt struck her, grabbed fists full of bedding, her knuckles growing white with the force of her grip. But her ass lifted, silently pleading for more and he gave it to her, brought the belt down time and time again until she was sobbing, on her knees, her legs parted and her hips canted in an invitation that was nearly impossible for him to resist.

His belly glistened wherever his cock head had touched, leaving wet kisses of arousal in its wake. He leaned down, rubbed his cheek against Marika's hot, reddened skin.

Her scent assailed him. Lush, inviting, a visceral call to taste, to mount.

He wanted to give in to her sultry summons. Wanted to kneel behind her, trail his fingers through her slit and exalt in how ready she was for him before bathing his cock in wetness then pushing inside her.

Tallis distanced himself instead. He took a step back from the bed, tossing the belt onto the mattress for later.

"You know I won't let you off so easily, Marika," he said and watched the mouth of her cunt close and open, made hungrier by the menacing purr of his voice.

Like a stripper who knew how to play for an audience, how to excite with her actions, Marika's knees slid across the bedding in a sensual, sexual split that left her slit exposed as her body lowered to the mattress, her actions forcing Tallis' hand to his cock. She took her time rolling to her back, meeting his eyes, the defiance still there despite the lashes he'd given her with the belt.

He growled — deeply, seriously — when her hands sought her breasts in a blatant attempt to divert and control him. "You're making it worse for yourself," he said. "Do you wish to be tied to the bed all night, denied both the pleasure I can give you and what you can gain from your own hand?"

The thought of denying himself the same pleasure sent agony pulsing through his cock. But too much was at stake for him to allow her the upper hand.

"I'll be good," she whispered, dark lashes hiding both her eyes and her thoughts.

"Show me."

It was sensual torment to watch her leave the bed, her movement feline, provocatively submissive. She knelt before him, feminine hands on his thighs, her touch that of a supplicant while the heated caress of her breath on his penis was a siren's promise of unparalleled ecstasy.

Tallis knew the danger of showing any weakness when she was on her knees in front of him, her sweet, torturous lips so close to his cock. He cautioned himself against speaking, but even as he told himself not to risk revealing how desperately he wanted her, his mouth was a traitor.

"Marika." It came out hoarse command and masculine plea, was punctuated by the throbbing of the veins on the underside of his penis, by the way his cock strained, bobbed as if trying to draw her attention to it.

She glanced up through dark eyelashes. Met his eyes as she closed the tiny distance between them.

Raw need twisted in his gut. Anticipation had his buttocks clenching and his thighs bunching. A guttural cry escaped when she lashed his cock with her hot, wet tongue.

Tallis reacted as she knew he would, showed her the dominance she craved. He speared his fingers in her hair, tightened his grip until she moaned. She kissed up his shaft with feverish intensity, one of her hands going to his testicles, fondling and petting while the other circled his cock and held it so she could take him into her mouth.

There was no stopping the jerk of his hips, the pistoning that followed as she sucked him. He praised her with words, with the sounds of his pleasure, reveled in how deeply she took him, in how thoroughly she loved him.

She took everything, clung to him desperately, her arms going around his waist when he came. And afterward she nuzzled and licked, kissed and sucked until he was hard again.

"I need you," she whispered, looking up at him with innocent, fawnlike eyes.

White heat filled Tallis' mind, eradicated all thought. It took him a moment to remember the fey-directed attack and his intention of getting Marika to agree to leave the area.

"Get on the bed," he said, her small smile telling him everything he needed to know. She hadn't truly relinquished her power, hadn't yet been loved thoroughly enough to accept his decision to leave.

He would force her if necessary, doing it for her own good. But he preferred that she leave willingly even though he understood her attraction to Xanthus.

She'd get over it once she'd accepted a different male into her bed. Then they'd return. This was home.

"Get on the bed," Tallis repeated, his cock bobbing, licking across his abdomen in a sensual caress as she obeyed, sprawling on top of the bed clothing like a well-loved courtesan.

"Like this?" Marika asked, her knees bent slightly, her legs splayed so he could see her slick inner thighs, her puffy cunt lips and glistening slit.

Tallis followed her onto bed with the lithe, predatory grace of the panther he could become. With practiced ease he gathered the supple belt he'd discarded earlier and bound her wrists together, then raised her arms above her head and tethered them to the headboard.

She whimpered, spread her legs further and Tallis settled on top of her, held her to the mattress with his weight, his pulsing cock hard against her erect clit. Before she could speak and tempt him into fucking her, he covered her lips with his, thrust his tongue into her mouth in a deep carnal kiss meant to reinforce his mastery over her.

Marika writhed underneath him, her hips lifting as she tried to position herself so he'd find her wet opening and slide inside her. He growled in warning, gave her more of his weight and slid his hardened cock back and forth over her clit until she was shaking, trembling, tears of need leaking from the corners of her eyes.

Tallis lifted his mouth away from hers, defenseless against her tears even when passion was their source. He rose onto his arms, nearly obeyed when she said his name, begged for him to fuck her.

"Agree to leave," he said, panting, icy-hot sensation shooting up his spine as he humped against her bare mound and tiny clit like a human schoolboy afraid of making a baby if he penetrated his girlfriend.

"No."

Marika's answer was whisper soft but it was a shouted challenge to his masculinity, to what made him Sjen. His movements grew faster, more forceful as he thrust against vulnerable, feminine flesh.

Tallis knew he should stop. He should roll away from her, withhold the pleasure she craved until she promised to obey him in this.

He should make her watch as he used his hand on his shaft, found release without her. But he couldn't. She was a drug as potent as any the human race had ever developed. She was an elixir as powerful as any created by wizard or elf or fey.

Tallis swallowed her cries as he continued to rub against her, denying them both the ultimate ecstasy of a true joining until finally she sobbed and shuddered violently, then went limp beneath him, soft and sated, though she whimpered with pleasure when he lost what little control remained and came, coating her belly and mound with his seed and marking her in the most primitive way as his.

Marika nuzzled Tallis, gave him small, coaxing kisses in a show of submission. She knew where his fierceness and need to dominate originated, and it humbled her. His desire to keep her safe sprang entirely from love, not because his fate was bound to hers.

"I love you," she whispered, her cunt spasming with the ache to feel him inside her, connected in a way that was both physical and spiritual.

Tallis captured her lips, consumed her with the passion of his kiss as he freed her arms and wrists. Her hands went immediately to his back, fingernails scraping lightly over heated skin.

He hardened against her, growled in warning though they both knew it was too late. She canted her hips and this time his cock found her opening.

They both moaned when he slid all the way in. He was hot steel, a throbbing vital presence.

"I need you," she whispered. "Please take care of me."

"Always," he said, once again settling his weight on her.

He recaptured her lips, his tongue mimicking the thrust of his cock. Deep. Slow. All consuming. Reality narrowing to the places they were joined, to the intimacy of shared breath and the feel of skin against skin. Time stopped until their movements become frenzied, an urgent, mindless rush toward a bliss that transcended the physical.

Marika found it first, crying out her pleasure and satisfaction. Doing it again when Tallis gave a guttural moan as the catlike spines on his penis descended and hot seed filled her channel.

For long moments afterward they lay together in contentment, their bodies touching, their limbs tangled as their breathing returned to normal. Marika smiled when Tallis began purring. She couldn't resist pressing a kiss to his chest.

The purr deepened before he rolled away and stood. He lifted her into his arms and she cuddled against him. Warmth pooled in her belly with the knowledge that once they got into the shower, he would insist on bathing her. "You spoil me."

"You're my world," Tallis said and it was as simple and complex as that.

He paused at the bathroom door. Their eyes met and she saw implacable resolve in his.

"I understand the attraction Xanthus holds for you, but it's too dangerous to remain here while the dragons and fey search for the wizard's cup. What happened at the beach could have ended badly. Queen Otthilde would make you a prisoner to her court if she discovered you were Drui. Or she might well have you killed. We need to leave, Marika, at least for a little while."

"I'll talk to Aislinn tomorrow about taking some time off," Marika said, knowing she'd talk to Aislinn about more than that and regretting not having confided in Aislinn earlier.

She had no idea whether Aislinn could see the lesser fey spirits, didn't know if Aislinn was protected against their mischief, though she suspected Aislinn was, given the dragon watchers and Aislinn's Elven heritage. Still, she wouldn't leave until she'd warned Aislinn about the fey. And beyond that, she wanted to talk to Aislinn about Xanthus. Even the thought of being away from him made her heart ache.

Chapter Five

෨

Marika saw the dragon as soon as she left her apartment. Red and orange energy spiked and shimmered around him despite his casual pose.

He was sitting in a lounge chair beside the pool, a cup of coffee on the ground next to him, his leg bent to provide a surface for the newspaper he was reading — or pretending to read. Dark shades hid his eyes but she felt his attention shift to her. This one she recognized, or thought she did. She'd seen him with Xanthus at least once.

Her heart pitched into a fast beat with the realization that he'd been sent to guard her. It was the only reason that made any sense. But it begged the question, had he seen Tallis in his human form the night before? Had he reported it to Xanthus?

She glanced down at Tallis in his favorite cat form, golden, like a miniature panther. His ears were pinned back and his stare baleful as looked at the dragon.

Marika bit her bottom lip. Indecision held her in its grip as her thoughts raced.

She hadn't forgotten her resolve to speak to Aislinn. If anything, the need to do it had just become more urgent.

Tallis was capable of forcibly taking her out of town — not that he'd need to physically restrain her to do it. More than once since they'd been together he'd sent her into complete oblivion with a shattering climax.

Xanthus was equally capable of sending her into unconsciousness and carting her off to the dragon realm. But he'd have to get her alone, in a place where sexual excitement would cause the hollow, unseen dragon spurs at his wrists to extend from their sheaths and fill with serum. He'd have to pierce her skin with them, and if the tales told around Drui campfires were truth instead of old wives' tales, the serum intensified orgasm.

Her cunt spasmed thinking about the dragon adaptation for rendering human females unconscious. She couldn't stop herself from imagining the spurs dragging over her skin as Xanthus thrust into her in a mating frenzy.

In the time before the exodus of the most powerful of the supernaturals, when dragons lived in rocky lairs accessible only by flying, the serum and its side effect of unconsciousness helped keep human women from dying of fright. But it also served a second a purpose. It altered human chemistry, changed it for conceiving a dragon's young.

Marika closed her eyes briefly. She tried to deflect the image of herself pregnant and the joy she'd see on Xanthus' face, but couldn't.

Because of the healing ability inherent in the Drui, there was no such thing as infertility among them. With or without the Chalice of Enos, regardless of the curse placed on the dragons by the long-dead wizard, if she paired with Xanthus, there would be children.

Another glance down at Tallis, and Marika made her decision. If she was right, the presence of the dragon lounging so casually by the pool meant she was guarded, which also meant she was safe from fey mischief.

Tallis was going to be angry with her. *Pissed* was the exact word.

She knew he intended to stick by her side today, guessed even now he was plotting to take her away, to have her wake up in bed with a shapeshifter of his acquaintance and accept him as her second mate.

Husband, she reminded herself. That's what the Drui called their permanent lovers, the term she'd always used until recently, when she'd been assaulted by dragon and Sjen pheromones.

Marika gave a sigh, hoping it sounded convincing, like someone who'd forgotten something instead of someone acting. She turned to the door and unlocked it, pushed it opened just a little bit, dropping her keys in the process.

Another sigh and she leaned over, trying to keep her intentions from transmitting to Tallis through body language. Even though his tail twitched and his eyes remained on the watching dragon, she knew Tallis was aware of every nuance when it came to her.

Marika scooped him up smoothly, quickly thrusting him through the narrow opening and closing the door. She felt the blaze of his fury and whispered, "I'll be safe. Stay in the apartment," as she surreptitiously drew a rune on the wood— enforcing her will on him before hurrying to Inner Magick.

* * * * *

She's just sealed her fate, Tallis thought, morphing from feline form to the human one he preferred. Muscles rippled as he paced the length of the apartment. He didn't bother to manifest clothing in the confines of his prison, not with images of punishing Marika for her trick cascading through his mind.

Visions of making her scream in orgasm before she tumbled into unconsciousness had his cock filling. She'd caught him by surprise, both last night when she refused to leave and this morning when she saw the dragon.

Claws extended in his fury. The cat-desire to rip and shred, to fight against being caged rode Tallis.

He should have acted yesterday, after visiting the VanDenbergh estate and being in the presence of so many dragons. He'd forgotten just how potent their heat and pheromones were, and now he couldn't afford to delay in the hopes of arranging a meeting with Severn Damek and gaining protection for her. He couldn't risk Xanthus would claim her for a mate or take her to dragon realm. Either would make her subject to dragon law.

Tallis' pacing turned into a prowl. Methodically he roamed the apartment, gathering the things they would need and packing them into a suitcase as his mind raced, analyzed, tried to determine where he wanted to take her, who he'd see her mated to so the threat Xanthus posed would be over.

They'd have to travel by car. If she fought him, it'd be too difficult to travel by air. That ruled out Scotland and a mating to a cat-sith. It also made South America and a jaguar shapeshifter more difficult to accomplish.

The majority of supernatural gateways led from the human world to those belonging to the dragon, fey, and elves. But there were a few scattered portals maintained by witches and guardians and shapeshifters for traveling from one place to another in this realm.

Tallis' footsteps slowed as he contemplated using them, sped up again as he discarded the idea as too risky. It would be impossible to hide either his nature or Marika's from someone powerful enough to hold and control a gateway.

His lips pulled back in a silent snarl. He should never have allowed her to go out with Xanthus in the first place. He'd thought—

No, he hadn't. His judgment had been affected by dragon pheromones—not Xanthus directly, but by what going out with him had done to Marika.

Tallis touched the woven collar around his neck. The need to please and protect Marika pulsed through him in equal measure to the lust that had his cock rigid.

White-fire streaked through his penis as he thought about the times she'd come home carrying another man's scent, her body taut with need, her cunt weeping for a cock to pierce her. The ache to be mated heightened her submissiveness, drew out his dominant nature. Each time she'd come home he'd made her touch herself, ordered her to say Xanthus' name as she came before he'd taken her himself.

He'd told himself he was helping her get over the dragon, ensuring when he mounted her, he'd fill her channel and her thoughts, be her entire world. But he'd been fooling himself, playing a sexual game because he longed for her to accept a second male in her bed. And in the process he'd reinforced the claim Xanthus had on her body, perhaps her heart.

With a snarl Tallis moved to the bed and sprawled across it, his hand going immediately to his cock, encircling it in a steel band of fingers. When he caught up to her...

His buttocks clenched as his hand moved upward on his shaft, enclosing the wet tip in a hard fist for an instant before sliding downward. It was too easy to imagine her slick, heated channel, her face as he held her wrists to the mattress and thrust into her, slowly at first, then faster.

A moan escaped, his hand serving as her channel, a substitute allowing his reality to blend with fantasy. In his mind's eye he saw her dark, dark eyes fill with a need only he could satisfy. He heard her whispered pleas in his mind, to let the spines on his penis descend and rake across her inner muscles.

His fist tightened on his cock to the point where pleasure and pain merged perfectly for him — and the fantasy changed. Another cock was inside Marika at the same time his was, making her already small channel even smaller, squeezing him until his only thought was to thrust faster and faster, to give her his seed.

Breath shuddered in and out of his lungs. The spines descended so each stroke, each time the edge of his hand struck them, torturous pleasure shot through Tallis, ripping away a little more of his control until finally there was none and he cried out Marika's name as semen coated his belly and chest.

* * * * *

Aislinn was in the back room, her face pale with exhaustion and worry, her eyebrows drawn together in intense concentration as she compared the necklace in her hand to the sketch on the workbench.

Marika's heart sank. She couldn't bother Aislinn with her troubles, not right now anyway. "That for a client?"

"For Sophie. She should be here any minute now."

As if on cue the chimes over the front door sounded. Marika's first instinct was to bolt from the shop to avoid seeing Xanthus.

He'd be with Sophie. Logic dictated it. The heat roaring through her body confirmed it.

Marika stiffened her spine. She was safe at Inner Magick. And what better place to start negotiations with Xanthus?

"Do you want me to send Sophie back?" Marika asked, turning away from Aislinn.

"Yes. Just her."

Marika pushed through the beaded strings separating the shop from the back room. Fire scorched her nerve endings when her eyes met Xanthus'.

Her mouth went suddenly dry. He knew about Tallis. It was there in every line of his body, in the fiery possessive heat of his eyes.

She licked her lips and saw him stiffen. Couldn't resist the impulse to look downward, to the thick, hard length of his cock pressed to the front of his jeans.

"Aislinn's in her workroom, Sophie. You're the only one she wants back there right now."

It was a testament to Xanthus' trust in Aislinn that he spared only a quick glance at the beaded strings serving as a doorway between the two rooms before returning his attention to Marika. Sophie disappeared from sight and Marika sought the protection of the counter, only to realize her mistake when

Xanthus followed her, trapping her in the small space between cash register and end wall.

He crowded her, the red-orange dragon energy and potent pheromones making her shiver. Arousal gushed from her slit, soaking her panties and coating her inner thighs.

Xanthus curled his arm around her possessively, pushing his hand beneath her loose shirt. His palm burned against her belly, sent spikes of desire straight to her clit.

"Do you love him?"

"Yes."

The answer was met by a low rumble, a barely human sound. "Tell me he satisfies you completely."

Her cunt spasmed in response to the challenge she heard in his voice. "I'll never leave him," she countered.

The rumble deepened, intensified as if he was fighting to maintain the illusion of being human, struggling to remember his duty to guard Sophie.

Marika shuddered when he forced her to lean forward over the counter. A whimper escaped, erotic fear coupled with exquisite need.

"Tell me he satisfies you completely," Xanthus repeated, using his free hand to jerk her short skirt up, leaving her exposed in sheer panties, making her feel vulnerable and powerful at the same time.

Rough jeans pressed against bare flesh and thin material. Fingers curled around her thigh, found the evidence of her need for him.

"Tell me, Marika."

"It's complicated."

His hand moved upward, cupping her mound so her clit throbbed against his palm. "You'll have to do better than that."

Xanthus applied pressure and she moaned, wanting his fingers to slide inside her panties, to slide inside her channel and relieve the pressure building inside her.

"If he satisfied you completely then you wouldn't be wet for me. You wouldn't have gone out with me."

Marika closed her eyes, tried to fight through the waves of desire, the nearly painful clenching of her cunt. There were tourists on the street, window-shopping, taking in the sights. A pause, a glance, and someone would see her through the glass front of the shop.

Reason tried to assert itself, but lost to an onslaught of fantasy — not of strangers watching her with Xanthus, but of Tallis watching. His hand gliding up and down his cock while another man took her. Xanthus doing the same.

The hand on her belly moved downward, reached the waistband of her panties. Marika's breath caught, anxious need building, anticipation held on a knife-edge of worry that her bare cunt wouldn't please him.

A shudder went through her when Xanthus' fingers slid beneath the elastic and over her fevered flesh. He purred with satisfaction when he encountered only smooth skin, the sound pure dragon, one she doubted he was aware of making.

The heat at her back intensified. His hips jerked subtly.

She quivered. Wondered if she'd have the will to stop him if he pushed her panties downward and unzipped his jeans.

Desperate need clawed through her, identical to what she felt for Tallis. Confirming what she'd come to believe, that somehow, someway she had to make it work with Xanthus.

His hand pushed further into her panties, his fingers reaching her clit before he stiffened with tension. A buzzing sounded in her ears, a drone she couldn't place until this rumbling purr became a frustrated groan and she realized the ring of his cell phone was muted.

"You're mine, Marika. This isn't finished between us," Xanthus said, cupping her, rubbing the wet swollen lips of her cunt with his fingers before pulling his hand from her panties.

He retrieved his phone, hissed as he checked the message then stroked his hand over her buttocks and tugged her skirt downward. "Severn's mother is approaching," he said, all traces of the lover gone. "Whatever happens, stay behind the counter."

Short moments later a female dragon entered the shop trailed by two men. Xanthus went rigid with the desire to attack, his sole focus on the men. They were lean and thin-faced, dark-eyed and reptilian, their signature energy black, toxic.

Marika didn't know what they were, only that they most likely originated in the dragon realm. They reminded her of the komodo dragons she'd seen when she traveled to Indonesia, creatures whose bites were as deadly as their physical attack.

Severn's mother oozed a different kind of toxicity. She took in Xanthus' protective stance, spared a dismissive glance at Marika before focusing on Xanthus and saying, "I see you are cursed with the same weakness my son is. In your case it is understandable. You come from a long line of deviant males and the weak females who allow themselves to be shared."

Revulsion showed in her face and laced her voice. But her words sent hope and happiness crashing through Marika. If what Severn's mother said was true...

Sophie and Aislinn emerged from the back. "I don't believe you'll find what you seek here," Aislinn said. "Perhaps I can direct you to a more suitable place?"

Fire flashed in Severn's mother's eyes but she didn't retreat from Inner Magick. She turned away from Aislinn and began examining a display of tarot cards.

Sophie headed toward the door. The tension rose immediately in Xanthus. He took a step forward, his obvious reluctance to leave her unprotected filling Marika's chest with hot emotion.

She wanted to press her lips to his and tell him not to worry. She wanted to hold him in her arms, in her body, to tell him about Tallis and voice the words she hadn't dared believe possible before — that she could belong to him as well as Tallis. But this wasn't the time or place.

Marika breathed a small sigh of relief when Sophie stopped, visibly stiffening her spine before turning away from the front door and going to the case displaying the runes. Some of the tension in Xanthus lessened, though Marika sensed his readiness to act if necessary.

Severn's mother moved to Sophie's side. They exchanged words Marika couldn't hear but from Sophie's expression, and from the way Severn's mother departed moments later with her guards, she thought Sophie had won the confrontation.

Sophie lingered in front of the rune sets only bit longer, then glanced at Xanthus and said, "I'm ready if you are."

Xanthus nodded. He turned to Marika and for the first time since she'd met him, she glimpsed uncertainty in his eyes. She could guess its cause, worry over what Severn's mother said, though the look was there and gone in an instant, the bold confidence of a male dragon quickly replacing it.

Marika placed her fingers over his mouth before he could say anything. "There's someone I want you to meet."

Heat flared between them. Her nipples hardened instantly and her cunt resumed its weeping cry for Xanthus' cock.

He tangled his fingers in her hair and leaned forward. Her fingers dropped away from his lips and he covered hers with a possessiveness that made her whimper and cling to him as they sealed their unspoken promise to be together with a deeply carnal kiss.

Chapter Six

ജ

"That kiss said the fight between you and Xanthus is over and you've made up," Aislinn said after Xanthus and Sophie left.

Marika worried her bottom lip as sudden doubt assailed her. Was it possible she'd misunderstood Severn's mother? Or worse, what if she was only repeating rumor, acting in spite because she was angry at her son for choosing Sophie as a mate? "Do you think it's true? What Severn's mother said about the men in Xanthus' family? Until she came in here I thought I might have to leave if I couldn't find a way to get Xanthus to accept another man in my life. I intended to talk to you about it when I got here, but you were busy."

"So Xanthus hasn't guessed there's someone else?"

"He knows." Marika clamped her thighs shut and only barely prevented a whimper from escaping as memories crowded in.

Xanthus asking, *Do you love him?* Xanthus cupping her bare mound, rubbing his palm against her clit, his voice the rumbling purr of a dragon as he demanded, challenged, *Tell me he satisfies you completely.*

"He knows," Marika repeated. "He knew even before I admitted it to him. This morning when I left my apartment there was a…"

A lifetime of caution trapped the words in Marika's throat. For an instant she fought against lessons learned in childhood and the survival habits necessary for the Drui youth-time spent wandering.

She found the courage to reveal herself by reminding herself of how much she already trusted Aislinn, and how this place had come to feel like home. "There was a male dragon lounging by the poolside. I recognized him. I've seen him with Xanthus. He probably belongs to Severn. I think he was guarding me, just as I've seen others guarding Inner Magick. I'm pretty sure the dragon at my apartment saw me with Tallis yesterday and told Xanthus."

Aislinn's smile made it easy for Marika to add, "I'm Drui. And you're elf."

"Half-elf," Aislinn corrected, shadows of pain in her face though it didn't reach her voice.

"You guessed?" Marika asked, remembering the day she came into Inner Magick as if drawn there by fate and asked about a job.

"For a time I lived in Elven-space. There was a Drui who came to the annual fair, a woman who chose freely to live among my mother's people. You remind me of her."

"Do you miss Elven-space?" Marika asked, responding to the sadness she saw in Aislinn and wondering if Aislinn chose to live in this realm or if she'd been banished from the place Elves called home because she was mixed-race.

Aislinn shook her head. "No. I don't belong there. When I didn't pass my grandfather's tests, failing to prove myself worthy in his eyes, it was almost a relief to be cast out and come back to a place I remembered being happy in. I've come to understand it's the heart that creates families, not ties of blood. And for whatever reason, my Elven gifts are actually stronger here than in Elven-space."

Marika covered Aislinn's hand with hers and squeezed. "I'm very glad you're in this realm, and that you hired me even though I suspect you didn't really need an assistant at the time." She grinned. "Of course, now you have Trace. And you *do* need someone to take care of the shop on those days when the uber-macho detective, who Sophie has so aptly nicknamed The Caveman, places you under house arrest so he can have you all to himself."

Aislinn blushed and laughed. "Dragon males aren't known for their civilized natures when it comes to their mates either."

Some of Marika's amusement slid away, replaced by her earlier worry. "Do you think Severn's mother was telling the truth? Have you ever heard of dragon males sharing a female?"

"I believe she was telling the truth. Pierce might be able to tell you if he's heard rumors about dragons sharing their females, but thanks to Severn's mother, now you can ask Xanthus directly. Though somehow that kiss before he left looked like it might be answer enough."

"You're right. I'm worrying for nothing because it seems too good to be true. Ever since I met him I've been trying to convince myself I couldn't be with him, that there was no future for us, and now suddenly, on the very day I though I was going to have to leave for a while, I find out everything is different than I thought it was. If he'd just told me... Or maybe if I'd told him about Tallis..."

Marika grimaced as she remembered her hasty decision to lock Tallis in the apartment. If she'd allowed him to accompany her to Inner Magick then he'd have overheard what Severn's mother said. Instead she now had an enraged, ultra-protective Sjen guardian to deal with in a very tricky situation.

She knew what was going to happen as soon as she walked into the apartment. He'd be on her in an instant.

Marika's cunt spasmed despite the seriousness of her problem. She imagined Tallis taking her. He'd be rough, aggressive, ripping her panties down and shoving her skirt up before she could get a word out.

If he worried she'd command him, he'd take her against the back of the door, covering her mouth with his to keep her from speaking. Or more likely, the cat's nature would assert itself and he'd take her on her hands and knees, shove himself inside her in a predatory claiming. Either way it'd be a hard, furious fuck, one meant to assert his dominance and leave her unconscious when she orgasmed.

"I've screwed up," Marika said, her mind scrambling for a way out of the mess. "I'd already decided to talk to you, maybe see if you could make a charm that would react in the presence of both Xanthus and Tallis so I could convince Xanthus that Tallis and I came as a package deal. But when I saw the dragon this morning, I panicked and locked Tallis in the apartment. I used a rune to keep him there. He's Sjen. Well, mostly Sjen now. I saved his life when he was in a feline form. In the process I changed him and also bound him to me. So instead of being a guardian spirit tied to a place, he's tied to me."

Aislinn indicated the phone sitting on the counter. "Call him."

"I can't. The only phone I have is my cell. Tallis is usually somewhere nearby. But if he's not and I need him, he knows it and comes to me." Marika nibbled on her bottom lip as her thoughts turned to Xanthus. What if he'd already agreed to share his mate with a male in the dragon realm? Xanthus had the same ability as Tallis to render her unconscious. The only thing stopping Xanthus from doing it was his duty to Severn. "Do you think the Chalice of Enos is going to surface again?"

"Yes. I'm working on something that may help the dragons recover it."

"Is that why there are more dragons guarding the store?" They'd been hard for Marika to miss, though she'd been grateful to see them in larger numbers since their presence had scared off the lesser fey who'd tried to harm her.

"Yes. I think a few of them are Severn's men. But most belong to Malik. Thankfully they're being very discreet and I'm being very careful. Trace hasn't noticed them watching the house or the shop and I'd like to keep it that way. One hint of danger —"

"And he'll put you in handcuffs and keep you at home."

Aislinn's blush was confession enough. She changed the subject by saying, "So you can see the fey when they're in their elemental form?"

Marika nodded. "Some of the lesser ones followed me when I left the store last night. They stirred up trouble. Tallis took care of it."

"Which is why he wants you to leave," Aislinn said.

"It was the last straw. Now he not only wants me to leave, he's determined I *will* leave. I can't go back to the apartment alone and showing up with Xanthus wouldn't be a good idea. I think I need a safe place to stay. Somewhere that could serve as neutral territory for when Xanthus and Tallis meet for the first time. We need to reach an agreement about where we're going to live. I want to stay here. This feels like home for me, but I have no idea what Xanthus' obligations are." Anxiety made her hand curl into a fist. "It seems crazy that I can trust Xanthus with my body and my heart, but I can't tell him I'm Drui until I know whether or not he's prepared to stay in this world."

"Not crazy," Aislinn said. "Smart. Dragons are ancient. They were the first supernatural beings to come into existence. Their laws are detailed and their politics complicated. Xanthus might not be free to follow only the dictates of his heart. That isn't to say you can't reach a compromise. It might be necessary for you and Tallis to form an alliance with one of the dragon princes in order to offset Xanthus' obligations, but where there's a will, there's a way."

The soft chime above the shop door had their attention shifting. Storm O'Malley stepped into the Inner Magick.

"This looks serious," Storm said, the instincts that had propelled her from beat cop to homicide cop kicking in.

Aislinn laughed. "It is. But you've got great timing. Now I know the perfect place for Marika to hide."

"Who's Marika hiding from? And why?" Storm asked as she crossed the shop to lean against the counter. Her pose was casual but there was no hiding the fact she was a cop through and through.

How she'd ended up "married" to two Sidhe princes amazed Marika, yet at the same time, it was a testament to how love knew no obstacles. If she'd only been as honest in her needs as Storm...

Marika shrugged the self-recrimination off. It was too late for regrets, but thankfully not too late to have both Xanthus and Tallis in her life.

"Xanthus to start with," Aislinn said. "Marika can't let him whisk her away to the dragon's realm until she introduces him to their third and the two men reach an accommodation about sharing her and about staying here."

Storm's face showed her surprise at the open discussion of the supernatural, though it quickly disappeared. "Two men?" she teased. "Double the pleasure but double the trouble."

Aislinn snickered. "You'd know."

"Guilty as charged," Storm said. She cocked her head and looked at Marika. "So who's the other one?"

"Tallis."

"Your cat?"

Marika bit her lip. Damn! She tried to be careful not to use his name when he was in cat form. Not because his name held power over him, but because Tallis liked variety. One day he might be Abyssinian or Siamese, another a nondescript gray tabby. It became hard to explain if *all* the cats seen with her were named Tallis.

"The cat is a secondary shape," Marika said, then felt compelled to add, "And he's not limited to a house-cat size. When it amuses him, he's a panther. But most of the time he's a man."

Storm gave a low whistle. "And you're hiding from him because?"

"The short version is he wants me to leave and he's perfectly capable of *making* me leave."

"Which is only part of the problem," Aislinn said. "The bigger issue is that she used a rune to trap him in her apartment."

Storm shook her head. "He's going to be one pissed kitty."

"That's why I need a neutral place." Marika grimaced. "And a brave friend to retrieve Tallis from the apartment and bring him to me so we can make up before Xanthus arrives on the scene."

Aislinn said, "*Treasure Hunter* would be the perfect place. If Marika takes the boat out into the ocean then Xanthus couldn't easily take her to the dragon realm portal when he catches up to her."

"What's to keep Tallis from heading to the Caribbean with her?" Storm asked.

"He won't," Marika said. "Tallis has waited for a long time for me to settle down in one place. He likes it here, and he'll accept Xanthus in our bed."

Storm frowned. "But will Xanthus accept Tallis? From what Pierce and Tristan have told me, dragons aren't keen on sharing."

"They're usually not," Aislinn said. "But it seems the males in Xanthus' family are an exception."

Storm shifted away from the counter. "Okay, then how about this for a plan? If you can spare Marika for a little while, the two of us can head over to Drake's Lair to make sure I still have access to *Treasure Hunter*. It's possible whoever lost the boat playing poker with Pierce wants a chance to win it back.

"Assuming the boat is still accessible, we'll swing by the marina so Marika can look things over before I bring her back here. Last I heard, Xanthus is still guarding Sophie. Marika should be safe enough from him until this thing with the Dragon's Cup is settled. So that leaves Tallis." Storm grinned. "If I open your apartment door, am I going to find a man, a panther, or a nice house cat?"

"A house cat. But it would be safer if you called me once you were outside my door. Tallis has excellent hearing. He won't suspect you know what he is. If he overhears us talking, and thinks you're there to get him and bring him to me, he'll behave." Marika nibbled on her bottom lip. "I think. I hope."

Storm snorted. "You're not the only one. What about the rune trapping him in the apartment?"

Marika reached for the small pad of paper next to the phone then picked up a pen. She drew two interlocking symbols before tearing the top sheet from the tablet and handing it to Storm. "As soon as you pass through the doorway, he'll be free to leave. He won't though, not if he believes you're retrieving him for me."

"Okay then, let's head to Drake's Lair. We can work out the timing on getting Tallis to the boat later."

* * * * *

Xanthus watched Sophie wade into the ocean. Tension and worry mounted with each step she took. He'd argued with her in the car, told her repeatedly that Severn wanted her to stay away from deep bodies of water. Unfortunately Severn hadn't instructed Sophie to allow Xanthus to drive the car, just as Severn hadn't authorized Xanthus to use force if necessary in order to keep Sophie out of the water.

His hands, and Severn's, were tied further by an inability to tell her *why* she shouldn't go in the water. She wasn't yet bound by magic to Severn, meaning they couldn't reveal the danger the fey represented to Sophie—especially those from Otthilde's court whose elements were air and water.

By the time they'd gotten to the beach it was too late to stop Sophie from doing as she wished. And though Xanthus didn't know the exact nature of the necklace Sophie got from Aislinn, he could sense the Elven magic and could guess Sophie's plunge into the surf had something to do with sealing a spell or binding the charm to her.

He trusted Aislinn completely, knew from the time he'd spent guarding her that she was loyal to her friends, gentle in nature and free of the Elven obsession with purity of blood. And beyond that, he doubted the fey could get to her, whispering their wishes and suggestions into her mind, as they could with the completely human.

The scowl on Xanthus' face deepened as he scanned the horizon. There was just the barest hint of fey magic.

It could be a harbinger of danger or it could be naturally occurring. Not all of the fey followed the Sidhe into the realm they created. Some, like his grandmother's family, remained in this world, though their magic was greatly diminished and they were more vulnerable to both human and supernatural attacks.

His attention shifted back to Sophie. She'd stopped where the water struck her at mid-thigh. As he'd suspected, she pulled the gift from Aislinn out of her pocket and dipped it into the ocean then pulled it out of the water.

Just as she clasped it around her neck fey magic burst over Xanthus and he heard the faint call of a woman's saying, "Help me."

"Sophie!" Xanthus yelled, plunging into the ocean without hesitation.

"Help me," the female voice cried again. It was low, just barely above the sound of the surf—a deadly trap for any human who answered it.

Fear seized him when Sophie ignored his call and took a step toward the cry for help, only to be pulled under. When she emerged from the water coughing and sputtering, he yelled Sophie's name again in a voice that demanded her attention.

She turned. "I'm okay but I think someone's in trouble. Did you hear a woman calling for help?"

"It's a trick of the wind and water."

"I'm pretty sure—" Her gaze went behind him, where he knew the rest of the hidden bodyguards had also raced forward, his actions making them aware of the threat though their lack of fey blood prevented them from seeing or hearing the fey trying to lure Sophie to a drowning death. "What's going on?"

"Severn's on his way back to the estate," Xanthus said. "Let's go."

"You're sure you didn't hear anyone calling for help?" Sophie asked, turning away from him and scanning the water.

Xanthus closed his hand around her arm in a firm grip. "There is no one out here in need of rescue except for you."

Sophie gave in a moment later and turned back toward the shore. "You can let go of my arm. I'm not going under again. You didn't need to wade in."

Xanthus snorted, relief restoring his sense of humor. "Severn might well kill me if I allowed anything to happen to you. Wet clothing is a small price to pay to ensure my continued good health."

Gratitude and affection toward Severn's mate swamped him. He'd never felt so torn between the requirements of honor and the call of his own heart as he had in that instant when it appeared Sophie would escape Inner Magick while the deadly gila-men were present. In both their reptilian and human forms, their bite was fatal to mortals, and though it would have been difficult to manage an *accidental* bite in Inner Magick, the thought of leaving Marika unguarded, especially after having Severn's mother note his interest in her…

"My thanks for not leaving Inner Magick before Severn's mother and her servants did." He squeezed Sophie's arm before releasing it.

"No problem. Are Aislinn and Marika safe?"

"Yes. Both Severn and Malik have men protecting Aislinn. Some of Severn's men also watch Marika when I'm not free to do so."

"Because of the Dragon's Cup?"

"Yes."

They reached the shore and paused to coax as much water out of their clothing as they could before going to the cherry-red sports car from Severn's collection. Sophie grimaced. "I hope we beat Severn home. I doubt he'd like to see us emerge from one of his toys like this."

"I'll drive fast," Xanthus said, holding his hand out for the key. He didn't intend to repeat his earlier mistake and allow Sophie control over their destination.

Sophie unlocked the passenger door then dropped the key into his palm. As she slid into the car, Xanthus' attention returned to the ocean and fury filled him at the sight of the woman now visible walking along the surf, her long black hair snapping behind her in the wind.

Sophie noticed her, too. When he was in the driver's seat she pointed and asked, "Do you know her?"

"Morgana."

"Is she the same woman who tried to kill Storm over Tristan?"

"Yes," Xanthus said, surprised Sophie knew the name. "What else do you know about Morgana?"

"Nothing, but I'm guessing she's related to Neryssa."

Xanthus gave her a quick look. "They're cousins and both dangerous. There's no love lost between them and Severn. The one they owe their allegiance to possessed the Chalice of Enos for a time. They will stop at nothing to reclaim it."

"So they're not dragons."

Shock made Xanthus jerk in reaction. He cut a look in her direction. Surely Severn hadn't revealed...

Sophie laughed and answered his unspoken question. "I'm a writer. I observe people for a living and put things together with the help of a very active imagination. I haven't figured it all out, I'm sure, but the dragon tattoo you guys all wear and the way you're competing for treasure practically screams *secret society*."

Xanthus chuckled, relieved and amused at the same time. "It's a good thing Severn found and claimed you. He's going to be the envy of many a dragon."

Sophie rolled her eyes. "You guys take the dragon thing to an extreme but somehow, at least in the men I've met so far, it's kind of fun. In the women on the other hand..." She gave a dramatic shudder. "I hope I'm not supposed to use Severn's mother and Audriss as role models."

Xanthus gave a shudder of his own, not all of it mock. "I think you'll find yourself imprisoned in a rocky lair high in the mountains if you do." He started the car's engine and a short time later they pulled into the garage.

With Sophie safely returned to Severn's compound, Xanthus thoughts returned to Marika. His penis hardened as he stripped out of his clothing and stepped underneath the shower. He imagined her kneeling in front of him, pressing kisses to the deep blue dragon streaked with silver and scarlet that rose from his hip to spread across abdomen, then taking his cock in her mouth as the other man in her life watched.

He cursed himself for not speaking openly with her about his need to share her. If he'd done he wouldn't have needed to find release with his own hand so often.

Xanthus wrapped his fingers around his cock. Stroked up and down.

He hoped the Dragon's Cup would soon be found and his duties to Severn set aside so he could go about the business of making Marika his mate and finally gaining an answer to the question of his own sexuality. Would he simply share her? Or would he share her lover as well?

Chapter Seven
ഗ

Marika rubbed damp palms against her skirt as she and Storm reached the front doors of Drake's Lair. It was a well-known club to humans and supernaturals alike, and a frequent target of law-enforcement raids though they'd yet to result in a single conviction for illegal gambling thanks to Pierce's faerie glamour.

She'd never dared enter it, wouldn't have dared it now except for Storm's presence at her side and then only because Storm was married to Pierce. Marika didn't believe in tempting the Fates unnecessarily. She might be guilty of playing with fire when it came to one particular dragon but she hadn't been crazy enough to enter a place overrun with them.

"Ready?" Storm asked, amusement as well as reassurance in her voice.

"As I'll ever be."

Storm opened the door and stepped inside, Marika right behind her. Opulent, that was the first word that came to Marika's mind.

The interior was like an old-fashioned gentleman's club. Darkly paneled walls. Plush carpeting and heavy, well-padded furniture. A hushed atmosphere of murmured conversation, the sound of a roulette wheel spinning somewhere in the distance and the clink of gambling chips.

"It's a pleasure to have you with us again," the dark-suited maître d' said to Storm, drawing Marika's attention to him and making her smile inwardly when he added, "I trust you're not on official business?"

Storm laughed. "And if I am? Would I catch Pierce involved in illegal gambling, Henri?"

"I fear you'd catch both Pierce and Tristan at the table. Shall I tell them you're here?"

"No, I'll surprise them and make sure they're not about to lose the club, the house, or the boat."

Henri laughed. "No fear of that. The last time I made my rounds Tristan and Pierce each boasted sizable winnings."

Storm shook her head and muttered, "Thank god I don't work Vice and this place doesn't fall within department jurisdiction."

Marika grinned, thinking Storm did a wonderful job of balancing being a cop against being married to Sidhe princes who didn't really consider themselves subject to human law. She followed as Storm led her through an area set aside for dining and drinking, with several cozy booths, perhaps there for private meetings, or maybe there for men who didn't want others looking at the females they'd brought to the club.

She could understand the sentiment. Though none of the dragons present stared openly at her, she felt their heated glances, could easily imagine them inhaling deeply and finding traces of arousal along with Xanthus' scent.

"If they offer you Dragon's Flame don't take it unless you like being scorched from the inside out," Storm warned as they stepped into the heart of club.

It was packed, every seat occupied. Most contained dragons, but Marika recognized several humans from their pictures in the newspaper or on television.

The sheer wealth casually on display was nearly overwhelming. Tables glittered with gold coins, were littered with sparkling gems and stacks of multicolored gaming chips.

Storm's hand circled Marika's arm, guiding her between the tables toward where Tristan and Pierce were playing poker with four old dragons. "It takes some getting used to. *They* take some getting used to."

"Yeah, I bet you had a hell of a time adjusting," Marika said, the monetary wealth paling in comparison to the sheer perfection of Storm's men sitting side by side.

There was a reason the Sidhe ruled the fey. They were elemental magic given beautiful form.

"You can look, but don't touch," Storm teased. "And since you're a friend, drooling is permissible, within reason, though you can bet word will get back to Xanthus if you do it."

"How do you get out of bed in the morning and leave for work?"

Tristan and Pierce were a matched pair, identical except for the color of their eyes. Together they were like a one-two punch.

"I admit, it doesn't get any easier as time goes by. With any luck, you'll soon have the same problem."

Both men rose as soon as Storm reached the table. Tristan kissed her first, then Pierce.

"Have you come to take us away in handcuffs?" Pierce asked, his voice holding sensual promise and wicked carnal knowledge as he let Storm go.

Marika's mouth nearly dropped open when Storm blushed slightly and said, "You wish."

"That he does," Tristan said. "Pierce is a glutton for punishment and as far as I can tell, never seems to learn his lesson. What brings the two of you to this den of thieves?"

"I told Marika she could borrow *Treasure Hunter* and take it out to sea." Storm made a show of looking at the mass of chips on the table in front of where Tristan and Pierce had been sitting. "I just wanted to make sure we still own it. It looks like we do."

Tristan flashed a smile and glanced at Pierce who said, "If Marika's plans include an outing with Xanthus, then *Sweet Surrender* would be the better choice." He dipped his hand into the pocket of his jeans and pulled out a set of keys. "I'd say the

Fates are at play once again. The yacht came into my possession only a short while ago. *Sweet Surrender* is anchored close by, at Pablo's Marina." Pierce offered the keys to Marika. "I know Xanthus can handle a yacht. I'm assuming you can too?"

Marika took the keys. "Yes."

Storm leaned forward, gave Tristan a thorough kiss before doing the same to Pierce. "You two behave yourselves and stay out of trouble."

"You could always pull out the handcuffs and take us into protective custody," Tristan teased.

"It may come to that. Later," Storm said, linking her arm through Marika's and leading her away from the table.

Marika wasn't surprised to see the dragon who'd been so casually lounging poolside at her apartment complex now leaning against the maître d's podium. "Do you know the guy with Henri?"

"Not by name. But he belongs to Severn. Which means you don't have to worry about Xanthus finding you."

A tremor went through Marika, anticipation and fear combined. "Xanthus finding me isn't the problem, it's what happens afterward that worries me."

Storm squeezed Marika's arm with hers. "What comes afterward is the ultimate fantasy. You, two men who you're crazy about and who are crazy about you. The three of you alone on a yacht. What could be better than that?"

* * * * *

Excitement whipped through Xanthus with the same force the wind turned his hair into a silver-white flag of victory as Hakon's speedboat raced toward the yacht in front of them. He could taste victory, could feel it in every cell of his body.

The Chalice of Enos would soon be in the possession of dragons. The answer to finding it had been in front of them all along, so obvious now in retrospect, and yet revealed only because Severn had claimed Sophie for a mate.

Xanthus glanced at where Sophie sat. Her hand was in Severn's, her face shining with the same excitement they all felt.

It was a tight fit, four dragon males and Sophie in the speedboat, but Xanthus thought it right that the princes Hakon and Malik be present, and he knew his own presence was necessary because of the fey.

Given the covenants, the dragons were at a distinct disadvantage surrounded by water and air. They were limited to their human forms while the fey were not, and though the lesser fey couldn't follow them quickly enough to take possession of the Chalice of Enos, Morgana and Neryssa could.

Xanthus lifted a pair of binoculars to his eyes. "*Fortune's Child* is straight ahead."

Hakon reduced their speed. Severn said, "Anything to be worried about, Xanthus?"

"No." At the moment they were free of the fey.

They drew closer to *Fortune's Child*. Hakon reduced their speed further to minimize the wake that would soon hit the power yacht.

"The cup is onboard *Fortune's Child*," Severn said. "I'd bet my fortune on it."

Malik nodded. "Before we get any closer, I suggest we agree on what we will offer Swain for it." He glanced at Sophie, then Severn. "It is a given we won't leave without the chalice but I imagine you've made concessions to your mate on how it's acquired."

Hakon chuckled. "Oh, how the mighty have fallen! And this is a fate you wish for yourself, Malik?" He turned his head slightly. "And you, Xanthus? Rumor has it your wings have been clipped as well."

Xanthus made a mock scowl at the dig, though his body responded as it always did with thoughts of Marika. His cock grew hard and the need to be with her scraped against nerve endings until they were raw.

"If it's any consolation to you guys," Sophie said, "one of my favorite sayings is, 'He who laughs last, laughs loudest'. It's followed by, 'What goes around, comes around'. I'll start racking my brain for someone to set Hakon up with. It might take me awhile, I'll have to find someone who deserves him— and I mean that in a *you poor woman* kind of way."

The men, including Hakon, laughed. Hakon said, "Your mate has sharp claws, my friend."

Severn nipped the side of Sophie's neck. "With any luck we'll be onboard *Fortune's Child* within minutes. Malik has a good point. I suggest our opening salvo be one million for the cup. That's the upper limit of what the insurance company would pay as a finder's fee."

"He'll want more," Malik said. "I'll match your offer if necessary."

"As will I," Hakon said. "But three should be our final offer. Any more and he loses the opportunity to negotiate with us. He has no right, either by law or custom, to the Dragon's Cup."

"Agreed," Severn said.

Malik nodded. "Agreed. Three million is a generous offer."

Hakon slowed the speedboat so the engine was a gurgle of sound as it drew within a few feet of the *Fortune's Child*. "Stuart Swain the illustrious fourth?" Hakon yelled.

"Who wants to know?" a man asked from the yacht's deck.

With a grand sweeping gesture, Hakon said, "Severn Damek and company, here to discuss a certain stolen artifact currently in your possession."

Stuart Swain threw back his head and laughed. "Your timing couldn't be more perfect. I'm in desperate need of an infusion of cash to fund my various vices. Let me cut the engine and drop the anchor."

It took only a few minutes for him to do it. The ocean was calm enough for Hakon to ease the speedboat alongside the platform at the back of the motor yacht. Between him and Stuart they quickly secured the boat.

Xanthus followed Malik and Hakon onboard and up to the deck. He scanned the horizon before nodding subtly to Severn that there was still no sign of the fey and it was safe for Sophie.

"Let us cut to the chase," Severn said to their host after he and Sophie were on deck and all of them sitting. "You are in possession of the cup that is erroneously known as the Chalice of Eros. My associates and I are prepared to offer one million dollars for it."

"It was insured for five million," Stuart said.

Severn casually picked Sophie's hand up and placed it on his thigh before covering it with his own. "True. But its disappearance is connected to a very high-profile murder. With the thief and murderer both dead, the police and district attorney would no doubt like a conviction, even if it's only for possession of stolen property. You learned of the cup's whereabouts from VanDenbergh's grandson?"

Stuart crossed his ankles. "Yes. We were lamenting the death of the old goat over a bottle of whisky, followed by a second, and perhaps even a third bottle. By then we'd moved on to considering which island to cruise to in order to gamble away V-Three's inheritance. Honey's name came up. One thing led to another and before I knew it V-Three was passed out in the stateroom of *VanDenbergh's Folly* and I was in possession of a very intriguing piece of information."

As in who VanDenbergh Senior's voluptuous playmate, Honey Mercante, had seen leaving with the Dragon's Cup on the day the old man was murdered, Xanthus thought, and a chance for Stuart to recover it on his own.

85

Stuart lifted a beer bottle from the table next to his chair and took a swallow. "Can I get you one?" When no one answered in the affirmative, Stuart said, "It seemed wise to lie low and keep the thing hidden until things settled down. I intended to share whatever proceeds I got from the sale of the chalice with V-Three, of course. But once it was in my possession it occurred to me that I was the one who'd taken all the risks in liberating it from the thief. And besides that, V-Three's prospects were vastly improved due to his inheritance." Stuart shrugged. "So here I sit, and here you sit. Five million would be a fair price. For that you get the chalice plus my silence — which is an important consideration given it's a stolen item and the police already know about your interest in it."

"Three million," Severn said.

Stuart took another pull from the beer bottle before setting it on the deck. "Once the money is placed in an offshore account, I'll give you the chalice."

Severn laughed. "We'll leave with the cup today."

"Do you think I'm crazy enough to keep it on *Fortune's Child*?"

Severn shrugged. "Crazy or clever or casual, it doesn't concern me. The cup is here and we will leave with it, peacefully or not. That's your choice."

"And my money?"

"Wired to an offshore account if that's what you prefer, though I would suggest an alternative."

"What?"

"You've heard of Drake's Lair?"

Stuart snorted. "Who hasn't?"

"It would be a simple matter to place the three million in an account there," Severn said. "You would be allowed to come and go from the club as you please, taking out what money you want in a form that suits you — gold, gems, cash — until the account is empty."

Stuart licked his lips. "Drake's Lair would serve only as a bank? Or would I be allowed to gamble there?"

"I offer access to the club, how you choose to use it is up to you."

"The money will be available this evening?"

"As soon as we reach land."

"Done." Stuart stood and disappeared below deck.

The training of a lifetime served Xanthus well, as it did the other dragons present. None of them reveled the excitement, the hope, the sheer happiness they felt. In a matter of moments, the Chalice of Enos would be in dragon possession for the first time since its creation.

Three million dollars was nothing to pay, though Xanthus' doubted any of the money would ever leave Drake's Lair. Stuart would find no shortage of offers to sit down at the card table for a game of poker. In just a few minutes —

Abruptly Xanthus felt the presence of powerful fey. He jerked his attention away from the door Stuart had disappeared through and scanned the horizon. The absence of an approaching boat told him the fey would strike in their elemental forms.

Malik and Hakon left their seats and positioned themselves to greet Stuart. Severn guided Sophie to her feet.

Stuart stepped through the door holding the Dragon's Cup, and for a split second Xanthus gave himself over to images of carrying it to Marika's lips then drinking from it himself, ensuring there would be offspring from their union.

The sense of approaching danger strengthened. Xanthus positioned himself at Sophie's other side, his hand curling around her arm just as a sharp, ice-cold wind swept across the deck.

"Time to leave," Severn said. "Get down to Hakon's boat, Sophie. Xanthus, go with her."

Fortune's Child rose on a sudden swell.

"Go," Severn said. "Hurry."

A small funnel cloud took shape on the deck. The boat continued to lift and fall unnaturally, making Xanthus' think both Morgana and Neryssa were present in their elemental forms.

Xanthus guided Sophie to the ladder, placing his body around hers, forming a protective cage so they climbed down in duet, his arms parallel to her head, his chest inches away from her back. When they got to the landing he gripped her arm to keep her from being knocked overboard and didn't release her until she was seated in the speedboat.

Mayhem reigned on the deck. Lounge chairs plunged to the water. Men cursed. The boat rose and fell and tipped, the smaller speedboat banging against *Fortune's Child*.

Hakon started down the ladder. Malik followed, gripping the Dragon's Cup as he maneuvered one-handed. Severn stood at the railing, waiting.

Another icy gust blasted them, timed perfectly with a violent pitch. Morgana and Neryssa working in perfect, devastating accord.

Malik slammed into *Fortune's Child*. Xanthus heard the sound of breaking bones as the dragon prince went limp.

The chalice was torn from Malik's grasp by wind but didn't drop downward. It was caught by a spray of water, a fey hand reaching up to capture and return it to Queen Otthilde's court.

In a nightmare Xanthus wasn't able to prevent, Sophie plunged into the water as the Dragon's Cup was carried under. "Guard Malik," Severn ordered before diving from the deck of the yacht.

Malik was conscious but dazed, concussed, his left arm useless as Hakon guided the other prince down the ladder and into Xanthus' care before following Sophie and Severn into the water. The wind ceased. The boats stilled as the battle for the chalice moved and was fought in the dark depths of the ocean.

Time slowed to an agonizing crawl for Xanthus. The lap of water against the boat and the sound of gulls abraded his nerves as he waited.

Sophie was still very mortal. If she was killed, drowned by Morgana and Neryssa... If the Dragon's Cup was lost...

Sophie broke the surface of the water, held in Severn's arms, the chalice still in her possession. Hakon appeared next to them.

Xanthus eased the boat over to where they treaded water. He expected censure in Severn's eyes for having failed to keep Sophie safe, but as Xanthus helped Severn into the boat, he didn't find it. Instead Severn's expression held a wealth of satisfaction and a hint of amusement.

"We will stop at Hakon's estate long enough for a shower and to change into dry clothing before taking the chalice to Drake's Lair," Severn said. "Once the cup is safely there, your service to me is complete and you are free to pursue you own pleasures. May you have better control over Marika than I have over Sophie."

Chapter Eight

ຂາ

Marika paced the yacht's deck. Her stomach was tied in knots. So much of this plan depended on timing *and* on masculine cooperation.

She caught her bottom lip between her teeth. This had seemed like such a good idea at Inner Magick, with Aislinn and Storm there, laughing and teasing, offering support. But now — alone, waiting, doubt gnawing at her, increasing with each ocean swell until she wondered if meeting both men in a restaurant wouldn't have been a better idea.

"No," she told herself. "This is the best way. Hopefully Xanthus and Tallis won't kill each other before they realize how perfect it is."

They'd be completely alone here. The master stateroom had a bed that practically screamed "made for orgies" and a sunken bathtub large enough to hold three people. There was a lounge with a great sound system, thick carpeting, an extra-wide sofa and plenty of other surfaces to accommodate multiple rounds of sweaty sex.

Marika's cunt spasmed just thinking about it. She gripped the deck railing and closed her eyes. She couldn't stop herself from imagining the three of them naked.

Arousal soaked her panties with thoughts of first Tallis, then Xanthus lying on top of her, thrusting their hot, hard cocks inside her and coming in a scorching rush of ecstasy. She pressed her thighs together, tightened her fingers on the railing to keep from sliding her hand beneath the waistband of her skirt and panties in order to pleasure herself.

A shudder went through her. Tallis loved to see her touch herself. Sometimes he made her bring herself to orgasm multiple times before he'd reward her with his mouth on her pussy, his tongue or penis in her channel.

He loved the bare, smooth skin of her cunt. Loved looking at it, touching it, seeing it touched. Told her in so many ways how much it pleased him.

A whimper escaped as Marika relived the moment in Inner Magick when Xanthus' fingers slid beneath the elastic of her panties. She heard again the dragon purr of satisfaction when he discovered the lack of pubic hair.

Her nipples tightened. She imagined undressing for him, seeing the possessiveness and hot desire in his eyes as he saw her naked for the first time and knew she belonged to him.

Would he strip for her? Or would he order her to undress him and pay homage with her hands and lips as she did it?

It was a game she sometimes played with Tallis. One that always led to her on her knees in front of him, pleasuring him with her mouth.

She'd seen Xanthus shirtless, seen the battle-posed dragon tattooed across his abdomen, a magical dark blue beast streaked with silver and scarlet. She'd longed to trace it with her fingers, to press kisses to it.

You come from a long line of deviant males and the weak females who allow themselves to be shared.

The voice of Severn's mother slid through Marika's thoughts, turning imagined pleasure into more carnal fantasies. In them Tallis and Xanthus wrestled on plush carpet, their cocks hard and leaking, the foreskins pulled back to reveal darkened tips, as they fought for the dominant position.

They were equally matched, utterly masculine. She couldn't imagine one of them truly mastering the other. But it excited her to picture their cocks touching, rubbing as they fought.

Would they take each other? Tallis was flexible in his sexuality. He would enjoy fucking Xanthus, and being fucked in return.

Is that what Severn's mother meant when she called Xanthus deviant? Or did she refer only to his desire to share his mate with another male?

Marika's cell phone rang, ending her speculation and making her heart race. She opened her eyes to the last moments of dusk and pulled her phone from the waistband of her skirt, saw it was Storm calling.

"I'm almost to your apartment," Storm said without prelude. "I just talked to Pierce. The Chalice of Enos and a standing-room-only crowd of dragons are on their way to Drake's Lair. You can bet money that as soon as the cup is safely there, Xanthus is going to be coming your way."

Marika's hand shook slightly, a tremble of nerves and anticipation as she forced self-doubt away. Tallis would forgive her. What she did, she did for both of them. "You'll call when you get to the apartment?"

Storm laughed. "Definitely. I'd prefer to find a nice little tame house cat instead of a thoroughly pissed panther when I open the door."

* * * * *

Tallis stopped pacing at the sound of approaching footsteps. They belonged to a female, the cadence and quality of them vaguely familiar, but not Marika's.

Claws slid in and out of their sheaths in aggravation. He tensed when the unknown woman stopped outside the apartment door.

Someone sent by the fey? Human lips pulled back in a feral smile. He considered taking the panther's form, but chose not to. At the moment he was more than ready for a good fight and to send a verbal message to anyone who thought they could harm Marika.

Tallis moved closer to the door. He positioned himself so the element of surprise was his. A key slid into the lock, sending a trickle of alarm through him along with worry that something had happened to Marika.

The woman paused before unlocking the door. Adrenaline spiked, rage nearly consuming him when he heard a familiar voice.

Storm. Someone Marika considered a friend.

Storm, who was married to Sidhe with ties to Queen Otthilde's court.

It took a minute for her words to penetrate the red haze generated by imagined betrayal, for his keen hearing to recognize Marika's voice coming through Storm's cell phone. "Okay, I'm here," Storm said. "Are you sure Tallis won't bolt out through the door when I open it?"

"No. He's pretty good about not trying to escape."

Tallis lifted his lip at Marika's comment. It was like waving a red flag in front of an enraged bull. Regardless of his form, he could see the magical rune she'd placed on the door to enforce her will and prevent his leaving the apartment.

With a thought he became the nondescript gray tabby he'd been when Storm had seen him. The apartment lock clicked and Storm opened the door cautiously, as if not quite trusting Marika's confident assertion about him not escaping.

Tallis lashed his tail in frustration. He wanted to demand answers, to find out where Marika was, but even from a distance she was imposing her will on him. Only the thought of exacting carnal punishment coupled with the knowledge she was safe kept him from becoming feral.

"Okay, I'm in. Your cat doesn't look too happy to see me. Either that or he's pissed that you aren't home yet. Are you sure he's going to let me catch him and bring him to you?"

Tallis stilled. Immense relief filled him, making him purr.

Storm's laugh told him she'd noted the change. Her next words confirmed it. "He must have heard your voice, Marika, either that or he understands what I'm saying. Now he's purring. And instead of baleful glances he actually looks friendly enough to pick up."

Tallis went to her, willing to play the tame kitty if it would get him to Marika faster, though he drew the line at rubbing against Storm's legs or standing on his hind legs. Claws dug into the carpet in frustration when Storm stepped past him, moving deeper into the apartment instead of leaning down and picking him up.

His gaze went to the doorway. Suspicion flared when he saw the protective rune no longer blazing there, but subsided. Marika had mostly likely traced a negating rune on her apartment key before giving it to Storm.

"There's a suitcase on the chair, I'm assuming you want me to bring it along with Tallis," Storm said from the bedroom.

Suspicion stirred to life again at the amusement Tallis heard in Storm's voice, but it was quickly eradicated, turned into heated lust and worried fury by Marika's reply. "Go ahead and bring it, though if this works out as planned I have a feeling I won't need clothes after Xanthus gets here."

Storm laughed. "I'll grab it."

She opened the closet, then retraced her steps, opened a second closet. "So where's the cat carrier?"

"You'll have to use a pillowcase."

Tallis couldn't prevent his lips from pulling back in a silent snarl. Storm earned points with him by saying, "You're kidding. You want me to put your cat in a sack?" though the amusement in her voice had deepened. "He's going to be royally pissed at you."

"I don't quite trust him to behave himself."

Tallis' eyes narrowed into menacing slits. Feline ears flattened against his skull. He didn't know what Marika was up to, but Xanthus being present made the situation dangerous and volatile.

Did she think that if her two men met, they'd reach a peaceful agreement? Did she think Xanthus—a male dragon in his prime—would willingly share a human he wanted to mate with?

Tallis hissed, his thoughts straying to the auction at the VanDenbergh estate, his conscience reminding him of how he'd basked in the potent heat and pheromones of the dragons attending. He had no one to blame but himself for this situation.

Despite her human years, Marika was young in comparison to him, young even among her own people. She was a Drui just reaching sexual maturity, only now ready to shed the wanderlust and settle in one place, to serve a territory.

It was natural she'd want the second male taking his place in her heart and her bed to be dominant and protective. Her mind might acknowledge that a dragon was a disastrous choice, but what defense did she have against her body's craving for him?

Storm pulled a pillowcase from the linen closet she was standing in front of and turned. "You sure about this? At the moment he looks like he might bite my hand off if I try picking him up."

"The only other choice is to leave him in the apartment," Marika said, "I'd rather have him here with me when Xanthus arrives."

Marika's words were spoken to Storm, but Tallis knew they were directed at him. Marika would expect him to be listening, had probably instructed Storm to call her when she reached the apartment. In the cat's form his hearing far surpassed a human's, something Marika was well aware of.

It took a supreme effort of will for Tallis to appear friendly. His only hope lay in cooperating, in getting to Marika as quickly as possible and taking her out of the area.

Storm opened the pillowcase and held it close to the ground. "Be a good kitty. Don't make me do this the hard way."

A growl escaped despite his best intentions. He knew why Marika wanted him contained. There were words she could speak that would have the same effect on him as the ward she'd traced on the door.

Tallis went into the pillowcase anyway. He promised himself that as soon as he and Marika were alone, he'd take control of the situation, though another growl escaped when Storm deftly tied the opening shut.

"Okay, he's bagged," Storm said, her continued amusement rubbing Tallis' fur the wrong way. "You want to talk to him?"

"Yes."

The cell phone was placed against the pillowcase. "I know you're pissed," Marika said. "Please don't be. I love you. This thing with Xanthus is going to work out. Trust me, Tallis."

He was helpless against her heartfelt pleading, couldn't find it in him to snarl and growl. Not that he'd let her escape punishment for her offenses. He wouldn't. He'd allow her a chance to explain her actions first. *Then* he would punish her.

The collar around his neck tingled, a sign she was about to utter a command he couldn't refuse to obey. But in an act of trust that soothed him further, she didn't follow through. Instead she said, "I'll see you in a few minutes," and Storm ended the call.

* * * * *

Excitement held Xanthus in its grip as he emerged from the car and joined the other bodyguards present, all of them there to guard the Dragon's Cup and celebrate as it was taken into Drake's Lair. In moments his liege service to Severn would be over for a time and his future with Marika would begin.

He glanced toward Pablo's Marina, remembered those last moments with Marika in Inner Magick, her whispered words, "There's someone I want you to meet," before their bodies melded and the their lips met, the unspoken promise to be together sealed with a deeply carnal kiss.

Worry for his family threatened to dampen his joy over the cup and Marika. But he knew if they were in this realm with him, they'd all urge him to claim his mate before turning his attention to his quest to be named Kirill's heir.

There was no guarantee he'd be named heir regardless of his feats or what magic-rich treasure he might find. There was nothing to prevent one of the others seeking the title from gaining it first.

His stomach tightened with the thought of the title — and more importantly, the valley and mountain region his distant relative controlled. It was between his family's ancestral lands and the portal gateway. Should it fall into the hands of a dragon like Severn's mother, who abhorred humans and fey and were intolerant of those who chose a different way of life, it would mean hardship for his family. His fey grandmother couldn't remain in the dragon realm continuously. She needed access to this world.

Xanthus forced his concerns away as Sophie and Severn arrived and got out of the sports car they were in. The princes, Hakon and Malik, pulled in behind them and did the same.

One of those serving Hakon opened the door to Drake's Lair as the Chalice of Enos was carried inside. The rest of the bodyguards, including Xanthus, followed, fanning out and encircling the crowd, containing it.

"Dragon's Flame for everyone who wishes it but especially for my mate," Severn said, his arm curled around Sophie's waist and holding her to him.

A uniformed waiter handed Xanthus a glass and he felt sheer happiness bubbling up inside him at having the privilege to serve Severn and be present for this moment in dragon history, to be part of the legend, even if only a small one.

Malik passed the Chalice of Enos to Severn and said, "May we all find the same good fortune as Severn has!"

Xanthus raised his glass and held it, waiting in silence with all those gathered as a waiter poured the fiery contents of a crystal glass into the Dragon's Cup.

Severn drank from the chalice then placed its rim at Sophie's lips. "May you all find the same good fortune as I have found!"

A cheer went up as Sophie took what was offered, not knowing as she did it how much her gesture symbolized the hopes and dreams of those male dragons present.

Xanthus emptied the Dragon's Flame in his glass and turned away from the scene, intent on heading toward the exit and the claiming of his own mate. Hakon's hand on his arm stopped him.

The dragon prince said, "Be careful. The fey have every reason to hate you. If not for you, they would have been able to attack without warning. Queen Otthilde isn't known for her kindness, or her graciousness in defeat. The fey will strike where you're weakest."

Xanthus acknowledged the warning with a nod. They'd be safe enough on *Sweet Surrender* tonight and he had no intention of leaving Marika's side, not until she was mated and taken to the dragon's realm, the bond sealed by magic.

* * * * *

Marika thought there were knots in her stomach *before*, but as she watched Storm guide the small motorboat toward *Sweet Surrender*, it felt like a macramé wall hanging was balled up in her guts. It would probably have been smarter to remain at the marina and spare Tallis the indignity of traveling in a pillowcase any longer than necessary. But getting the yacht anchored in a romantic cove so they wouldn't have to deal with it had seemed like a good idea.

Her hands tightened on the railing and her heart thundered in her chest. It wasn't like her to agonize over decisions and second-guess herself.

Marika grimaced. Maybe it came with the territory and the whole "settling down" thing. If so, then no wonder the Drui were slow to mature! The years when she was footloose and fancy-free were all about *no worries, no problems*, a heaven compared to the hell of constantly feeling confused and out of control.

"I'm betting Xanthus will be waiting at the dock to claim this boat when I get back," Storm said, easing the craft next to the back of the yacht and cutting the motor.

"Thanks for everything."

Storm grinned. "Oh, it's going to cost you. Next girls' night out, we'll expect a full report and a very detailed accounting of the events transpiring on *Sweet Surrender*." She picked the suitcase up and handed it to Marika. "Your luggage, not that you're likely to need clothes."

Marika laughed despite her mounting anxiety. She took the suitcase and set it down on the small landing platform.

Storm hefted the pillowcase, its opening knotted shut. "Your cat, who will hopefully understand this has all been done with his best interests at heart."

Marika took the pillowcase containing Tallis and set it down next to the suitcase. If there was more time, she'd take Tallis to the stateroom and strip so when he changed form he could immediately punish her and be done with it. But they didn't have that kind of time, not if Xanthus might show up at any moment. Neither of them had any idea how that particular dragon male would react if he found her tethered to the bed or being spanked.

With an amused smile and a quick wave, Storm pushed off from the yacht. Marika waited for her to get out of sight before kneeling to free Tallis.

She didn't plead or cajole, beg or try to further explain her actions as she unknotted the pillowcase. The most important words had already been said, when Storm held the phone against the pillowcase. And beyond that, she and Tallis had years of being together, a trust between them that it would be nearly impossible to destroy.

He changed the instant he was free of the material, looked every bit the irate man and pissed-off feline. His glare was scorching, his lips curled in a snarl. But his fingers were a gentle shackle around her wrists when he reached down and pulled her to her feet.

"What happened with Xanthus?" he asked, holding her tightly to his body with her arms locked behind her back.

The doubt and worry fell away with the feel of his hard cock against her mound. She pressed her mouth to his, nibbled and ran her tongue along the seam of his lips in supplication until he kissed her.

Tallis growled, a fierce sound that made her cunt lips part and her legs grow weak. He thrust his tongue into her mouth aggressively, vented his aggravation by dominating her thoroughly, making her whimper and melt against him in complete submission.

Slowly he gentled. He released her arms and murmured his pleasure when they immediately went around his neck. His hands smoothed over her buttocks, her thighs, before traveling upward, underneath her skirt.

His purr when he discovered bare skin made Marika tremble. She whispered *please* when he lifted his mouth from hers, wanting him to pull her skirt up and take her where they stood.

"Is that how you want Xanthus to find us?" Tallis asked, masculine satisfaction in his voice.

"I don't care."

His lips captured hers again. His hand moved to her hips and his thigh pushed in between hers.

She was beyond caring. Relief and desire mingled, fed her need to be close to Tallis, to be completely reconciled with him.

Marika rubbed and thrust her stiffened clit against the hard muscle of his thigh, panted and moaned until finally she found what she was after and cried out in release.

Tallis stroked her back, her buttocks. He purred deep in his chest and throat as he held her, letting her come back to him gently and find only safety.

He adored her. Loved her beyond measure. It was impossible to stay mad at her, though he would still insist on punishing her for the indignities he'd endured because of her.

"What happened with Xanthus?" he asked again, his lips closing around her earlobe, sucking, making her moan and shiver.

"It wasn't so much what happened with him, but what happened at Inner Magick. Severn Damek's mother came by when Xanthus was there. She saw us together and struck out at him, probably because she hates it that Severn's chosen Sophie for a mate. She said Xanthus came from a long line of deviant males and the weak females who allow themselves to be shared. He didn't deny it. And he already knew about you. Before he left I told him there was someone I wanted him to meet. He seemed accepting of it."

Tallis speared his fingers through Marika's hair and held her face away from his. Their eyes met and held. "I won't say no to him. But promise me you'll let me be the one to decide when the time is right to reveal what we are to him."

"I promise," she said, turning her head slightly to rub her cheek against his palm.

Tallis leaned in and took her mouth in a gentle kiss. The way she became soft and submissive against him, the absolute trust she placed him, were always his undoing.

"You're my world."

Her lips curved against his. Her scent intensified. "I think maybe it's time to expand your world."

The sound of a boat's engine came into focus. Instinctively Tallis' hands left Marika's hair and traveled downward, not stopping until they'd settled possessively at her waist.

Her earlier plea to be fucked whipped through his mind. He'd thought it unwise then, but now, as Xanthus drew closer, Tallis considered lifting her skirt and pressing her against the side of the yacht, establishing his claim to her in a way the dragon would understand.

A growl escaped. Tallis couldn't prevent it. Fighting for the right to mate was encoded in the cat's genes.

"Let's wait for Xanthus on the deck," Marika said, but didn't make the mistake of trying to pull away from him.

Tallis fought for control of the primitive urges and conflicting desires. Slowly Sjen instincts overrode the cat's. He released Marika. "Go," he said, reaching for the suitcase and discarded pillowcase.

Chapter Nine

❧

Xanthus rounded the shore and found *Sweet Surrender* anchored where he expected it to be. His attention went to Marika first. She was on deck, waiting for him, finally his to claim. Her hands rested against the rail, a gentle breeze pulling her hair away from her face and making her short skirt flutter.

His chest expanded with longing and heat. It seemed like he'd wanted her for a lifetime, hungered for an eternity for the chance to touch and make love to her. Thoughts of their last encounter at Inner Magick crowded in, only instead of seeing her bent over the counter, images of her gripping the railing as he took her were superimposed on his fantasies. For long moments his eyes lingered on her. But then his sense of humor asserted itself and he called himself a coward for not looking at the man next to her.

Xanthus' attention shifted and his body hardened further in reaction, giving him the answer to his long-asked question. He knew in a heartbeat that should Marika's other lover desire it, they would become lovers as well.

Dragon heat burned through his veins and his cock. It was an effort to keep himself from opening the front of his jeans and freeing his penis in a primitive display of masculinity.

Marika was trembling with need by the time Xanthus secured the smaller boat and climbed the ladder to the deck. Her nipples were hard points against the front of her blouse, her inner thighs wet.

"This is Tallis," she said, her womb fluttering at the bold, predatory way the two men sized each other up, as if they might circle and fight to determine which one would fuck her first, or fight until the winner mounted the loser.

Neither man offered his hand. Neither spoke verbally though there was a silent conversation, a fierce masculine communication taking place.

Her heart skipped erratically, a rapid dance that made her want to wedge herself between the two men and ease the tension. A small whimper escaped and Xanthus' nostrils flared—in reaction to her, or to some unspoken agreement he and Tallis had reached, Marika didn't know, but lust and relief entwined when Tallis' said, "Welcome Xanthus properly, Marika. On your knees."

She sank gracefully to her knees, committing every nuance of Xanthus' expression to memory. His face held a hungry willingness to play the games of dominance and submission she and Tallis enjoyed.

Marika leaned forward, rubbed her cheek against the hard ridge of his jeans-covered erection and was rewarded by a low moan, a subtle jerk of his hips. She pressed a kiss to the front of his jeans, ran her hands up hard, tense thighs but didn't stop when she got to his waistband.

Instead she tugged his shirt out of his pants and pushed it upward, uncovering the dragon tattoo that rose from his hip and stretched across his taut abdomen, a fierce dark blue creature streaked with scarlet and silver. "I wanted to do this the first time I saw it," she admitted, tracing the dragon with her tongue. Pressing kisses to it. Sucking and using her teeth, leaving no section of it unexplored, unclaimed.

Xanthus' breathing grew harsher. Fingers speared through her hair. "Enough," he said.

She glanced up at Xanthus through lowered lashes and obeyed. Her cunt lips were swollen, pulsing as if her heart beat between her thighs. Liquid heat slid past the hem of skirt. She knew it would be visible to Tallis in the moonlight, knew that both men were being swamped with the scent of her readiness.

Marika's fingers curled over Xanthus' waistband. When he didn't protest she grew bolder, stroking her thumbs over the thick bulge of his erection.

A spike of heat shot through her clit when she encountered the wet spot at the front of his pants, the evidence of his excited desire. His hands circled her wrists, manacling them. His low growl made her shiver with erotic fear and heated need.

Xanthus squeezed Marika's wrists in warning as he fought to remain in control of both dragon magic and fey glamour. How many times since meeting her had he fantasized about this moment, when she knelt before him, paid homage to the dragon part of him before taking his cock in her mouth? How many times had he woken, belly wet with his own come, after imagining her lips and tongue pleasuring him?

He shuddered, panted, felt Tallis' eyes on him, burning with challenge, daring him to unzip his fly and present Marika with his penis. It was as if Tallis somehow knew the human form was secondary, a magic construct containing a being not human, as if Tallis knew few dragon males could hide the true size of their cocks or the twin rings of thick cartilage circling beneath the head when a female's mouth was involved.

Xanthus' bared his teeth at Tallis and was met with an answering flash of white, the display of sexual aggression heightening the anticipation and lust, pushing Xanthus to dare what few pureblooded male dragons would attempt with a human female who was neither mated nor aware of the existence of supernatural beings. His fey blood gave him an advantage in this realm, the added control necessary to appear completely human. He unbuttoned his pants and slid the zipper down, freeing his cock.

His buttocks clenched as he curled his fingers around his penis, slid his hand up and down on his shaft in both offering and challenge. He felt immense satisfaction at the sound of Marika's low moan of appreciation and the liquid heat in

Tallis' eyes as he answered the challenge and freed his own penis to masturbate while Marika took Xanthus' cock in her mouth.

With another baring of teeth, Xanthus turned his attention to Marika. White-fire raced up his spine at the sight of her kneeling submissively in front of him, his at last.

She'd consumed his thoughts, made him struggle to retain his honor and complete his duty to Severn. From the first moment he'd seen her, his heart and body longed to do nothing but pursue her.

His hands dropped away from his cock. He felt a faint tingling at his wrists, where the hidden spurs waited to emerge from their sheaths and fill with serum. He ached for the moment when he could rake them across Marika's flesh and start the process of making her a true dragon mate.

Tallis' presence complicated things—or might have, if Xanthus didn't know already that before this night was done, he would take Tallis, perhaps be taken by him. The end result would be the same, Tallis would feel the rake of dragon spurs first, and while he was unconscious, Marika would be left with only one male to concentrate her attentions on.

Xanthus widened his stance, balling his hands into fists in a shoring up of his control as he saw the small tremors shaking Marika, the need-filled eyes pleading with him to let her love him with her lips and tongue.

"Take me in your mouth, Marika," he said, unable to keep his hips from jerking when delicate fingers gripped his cock and a feminine hand cupped his testicles.

A groan escaped, a pant. He suspected he was growling but he couldn't hear it for the thundering roar of his heart. Couldn't have stopped it anyway when it was taking all of his concentration to remain human in appearance.

Marika might be submissive but she was well aware of the power she held, had probably learned it as she knelt before Tallis and was given the same command. Her mouth was wicked, creating a torment of sensation that had Xanthus clenching his buttocks and spearing his fingers through her hair in desperation as she kissed and sucked along his shaft.

Her tongue punished as it explored, and he quivered, imagining her licking over the hard ridges of his dragon's cock. He should have known she wouldn't obey, that she wouldn't immediately take him into her mouth. He should have guessed, but it was too late to enforce his will, to pull away and punish her.

"Marika." Order and plea blended in his voice. His fingers tightened on her hair. Hers tightened on his sac.

Xanthus grew harder, larger. The dragon magic and fey glamour giving way to reveal his true size though not the distinctive ridges, the deep red tip of his penis glistening from the steady escape of arousal.

He changed the angle of his body while holding her in position, cried out in guttural triumph when his cock breached the seam of her lips and was welcomed into the heaven of her mouth. Nothing in his life had prepared him for the pleasure he found as her tongue laved him and her lips pulled on him.

It was different with a mate. How often had he heard that from his father and grandfather, from the men they shared their mates with? How often had he doubted?

No longer.

Xanthus closed his eyes, acknowledging his defenselessness when it came to Marika. Understanding in that instant what an act of trust it was to give himself over completely while in the presence of Tallis. The depth of his need made him vulnerable to attack but he couldn't care.

"I've dreamed of this," he whispered, hands roaming, tugging at her hair, caressing her face and cupping her neck as his hips danced to the rhythm she set with each suck, each lash of her tongue.

Helpless. He was completely helpless against her. A dragon tamed, wanting only to behave so she'd continue to welcome him in her mouth.

Her hands tightened, stroked, squeezed in the perfect blending of pain and pleasure, promise and denial. His testicles grew heavier, his cock throbbed, his world reduced to white-hot need and Marika.

He quivered under her touch. Could hardly contain the dragon fire and song longing to escape.

"Take me deeper," he said, prepared to beg, *willing* to beg—though he would return the favor, was already looking forward to hearing her plead as he loved her with his mouth and hands and cock.

This time she obeyed, took him deeper than he thought a human capable of. What little control he possessed dissolved with the working of her throat. He thrust mindlessly, trusting her to control the depth, trusting Tallis to intervene if necessary to prevent Marika from being hurt.

It was a frenzied rush to ecstasy. A fury of lust that could only find release one way—and did—with violent, lava-hot jets of semen and the satisfaction of having his female keep sucking even after he'd spent and softened.

Love and adoration filled Xanthus, a flush of happiness as he looked down at Marika. He was hardening again with her ministrations, with the small mews of need and pleasure she was making and the way she clung him, her scent an aphrodisiac.

"I'll take care of you," Xanthus said, easing her away from his cock, his attention finally leaving Marika and finding Tallis.

Feral eyes greeted him, a cock that rivaled his own in size, making Xanthus wonder if Tallis was fully human. But when he focused, he found no fey or dragon energy, no shapeshifter heat surrounding Marika's other mate. He found only raw hunger and the carnal intensity of a dominant male.

Humor returned to Xanthus, the gift of having been raised in an ancestral lair not purely dragon and having lived among humans for a while. No doubt he was lucky Tallis hadn't pounced.

The sight of Marika with Tallis' cock in her mouth would make him want to mount Tallis and prove himself. He imagined Tallis felt the same. Knew they were both waiting until Marika was thoroughly satisfied before exploring what pleasure they might find with each other.

Xanthus picked Marika up and carried her to the stateroom, set her on her feet in the middle of a luxurious carpet. Tallis stopped next him, their shoulders nearly touching, their heat and desire mingling, focused on the woman who stood in front of them. Theirs to share, to protect, to love.

"Remove your clothing," Xanthus said, taking himself in hand as Tallis did the same.

Marika trembled, burned with the need to bare herself for them, to have them touch and pet her, press their bodies to hers and slide their cocks into her. Her skirt dropped to the floor and their darkened eyes praised her, made her clit throb as it stood at attention, begging for their hands and mouths.

She kicked off the dainty sandals she'd been wearing, her fingers hesitating at the front of her shirt with shy insecurity. Her breasts were small, nonexistent compared to those of most Drui.

Tallis' eyes narrowed in warning. His lips pulled back in a silent snarl, a promise of punishment if she doubted her appeal. Arousal gushed from her slit in reaction, her sheath spasming as she felt the phantom sting of his palm against her bare mound, the kisses that always came afterward.

Marika unbuttoned her shirt and shrugged it off so she was standing fully naked before them, vulnerable. She waited for their command, her need for them making her truly submissive.

There were no words exchanged. And yet already Xanthus and Tallis were in sync. They shed their clothing in a perfectly choreographed move and came to her, Tallis at her front, Xanthus at her back.

Tallis' hands gripped her hips as he claimed her mouth in a carnal kiss, tasting Xanthus on her. Xanthus' cock pressed to the seam of her buttocks. His hands cupped her breasts possessively, the palms rubbing over her nipples as his lips trailed kisses over her shoulder, settled on the scar she bore from Tallis' repeated matings and bit, leaving her helpless, boneless.

They took her to the rug, plush carpet replacing dragon heat at her back. Tallis' mouth on hers kept her from begging with her voice. But she found another way. With the arch of her back. The splaying of her thighs. With hands that tangled in Xanthus' long silver-blond hair and urged him downward.

She hurt. She ached. The hunger gripping her was worse than anything she'd ever experienced, her body and soul and heart recognizing the importance of both Xanthus and Tallis being with her.

Tears escaped. She sobbed, cried into Tallis' mouth when Xanthus' tongue laved a hardened nipple before he took it between his lips, then his teeth. Tallis' fingers found her other nipple, squeezed and tugged with the same merciless rhythm as Xanthus suckled.

Please. The word was a constant chant in her mind. It screamed from every cell as she writhed and twisted, tried to find relief with her own hand, only to be stopped.

"No," Tallis growled, lifting his mouth from hers, forcing her arms above her head so he could pin her wrists to the carpet.

"Please let me come," she whispered. "I'll do anything you want afterward."

"Ask your other mate," Tallis said.

Marika's eyes sought Xanthus'. She wouldn't blame him for making her suffer for all the times she'd gone out with him, ensuring each time she'd done it that they would be in a place where he couldn't do more than casually kiss and touch her, then going home to Tallis.

"Please," she whispered, begging for his forgiveness and his understanding, pleading for him to take what belonged to him.

Xanthus was helpless to resist her. He knew he should punish her, take her to the brink of orgasm repeatedly and then deny her. But he wouldn't. He couldn't.

She was everything he'd dreamed of, soft and submissive, beautifully feminine. His, and willing to be shared.

He leaned down and claimed her lips, felt deep, primitive satisfaction at the way she tasted of dragon seed and Tallis. It excited him to have her wrists held down by another male, to have another man witness her claiming and hear her whimpers and screams.

Xanthus left her mouth and kissed downward, licking and sucking at dusky nipples before exploring her navel with his tongue. She quivered, lifted her hips in an effort to hurry him to the place between her thighs. He bit the soft flesh of her abdomen in warning.

Her scent and heat swamped him. It threatened his control so that for long moments he nuzzled and caressed her belly as he fought to keep the human form.

Loving her was torture. He wanted to reveal himself, to have her accept the dragon and the man, to take her as both.

Images of doing it, covering her and thrusting into her wet heat in his dragon form nearly undid him. White fire burned along his spine with the phantom rise of the dragon crest he had in his first form. Quick hard pulses through his cock made his hips jerk, warned that he'd be reduced to air humping if he didn't mount Marika soon.

Xanthus growled and held her thighs open, ate her bare pussy with his eyes. He'd been obsessed with thoughts of it since bending her over the counter at Inner Magick and discovering only smooth flesh when he slid his hand beneath the waistband of her panties.

No fantasy could compare with the reality of petal-soft skin and dewy, parted cunt lips. He'd be lucky if he didn't come at the first taste of her, with the first tightening of her sheath on his tongue.

Xanthus' palms glided up her thighs, over slick arousal and trembling flesh. "Everything about you is beautiful," he said, hardly recognizing his own voice.

His hands framed her mound. His thumbs stroked her swollen labia and the glistening female flesh between her cunt lips darkened with his touch, her opening spasming in invitation and need. He memorized every curve and fold, burned the image of her delicate clit with its tiny exposed head into his mind.

His sac hung heavy and full underneath a cock that ached. Hunger clawed in his belly and chest, threatening to peel away human illusion and free the dragon.

Xanthus leaned forward, pressed his lips to her cunt and was immediately lost to sensation. All thought left him. There was only desire, the need to taste and claim, to suck and kiss, and finally to thrust his tongue into her channel over and over again as she writhed violently, held to the floor by both her mates.

The sound of her pleasure beat on him. Her screams sheered away the thin veneer of a civilized man he wore in the human realm.

Dragon instinct dominated, insisting she climax for a second time, then a third. His primal nature only gentled when she lay completely sated, her limbs lax, her body seemingly boneless.

Even then Xanthus lingered between her thighs, inhaling her, nuzzling her, imprinting her in every cell of his being. His need to fuck her held in abeyance because of the exquisite pleasure he experienced at being able to finally love her in any manner he wished.

In the dragon realm his lair was lined with gems forming a glittering bed. He could lie upon them for hours in his first form, entranced by their warmth and smooth surfaces, by their beauty. But they paled in comparison to Marika. They were worthless trinkets against the priceless treasure of a mate, especially this one.

Xanthus would have stayed longer between her thighs, luxuriating in her, the beast content. Movement drew his face away from Marika's cunt, the phantom crest flaring along his spine when he was greeted with a snarl, a challenge by Tallis. "Take her now or I will."

Xanthus reacted without thinking. His arm curled around Marika's waist, easily lifting and turning her, repositioning her so she was on her hands and knees.

Lust flashed through him when she went to her elbows, canting her hips to tempt him with her slit. He pressed his penis to her entrance, forged all the way, finally able to let the magic concealing the ridges fade.

It thrilled him to see Marika's fingers tighten on the carpet. To have her rock back and forth on his cock, to hear her say. "Please, Xanthus, please fuck me."

Despite knowing and accepting he'd share her with another male, a silent dragon's roar rumbled through Xanthus. A single word, repeated with each heartbeat. *Mine!*

Xanthus held Tallis' stare, met the challenge and offered one of his own. He began thrusting, the thick rings beneath the head of his penis making Marika pant and cry out, stimulating and pleasuring her in a way no human male could.

Chapter Ten

❧

Tallis purred, basking in pheromones and lust and dragon heat. He stroked his cock. Slowing, tightening his grip to prevent himself from coming even as Xanthus' bit Marika's shoulder and the dragon's hips moved in a frenzied rush to orgasm.

The air shimmed dark blue with streaks of scarlet and silver. Dragon colors. Xanthus losing a measure of control in the instant his seed poured into Marika for the first time. Dragon magic flowing into Tallis and making him stronger.

Perfect. It was so perfect Tallis struggled to remember why he'd doubted the rightness of Xanthus as a second mate.

He closed his eyes and soaked in the dragon energy. Felt the runes in the braided collar around his neck heat and spark with dragon fire, no doubt casting a glow and serving to allay Xanthus' fears should he suddenly worry he'd accidentally revealed himself as supernatural at the point of orgasm.

Tallis rarely thought of the time when he'd been pure Sjen. In those days he'd been held to a single place by genetic inclination, trapped in a vast territory, his strength ebbing and flowing as natural magic moved from one place to the other, built up and dissipated in a world that had lost much when the dragons and elves and most powerful fey left it.

His purr deepened and his cock pulsed against his palm as magic poured into him, dragon and Drui, a potent cocktail fueled by lust. He touched the collar that not only hid his nature from others but kept him anchored to Marika. For the first time since she saved his life, he knew he could remove it without the risk of fading into oblivion. But he wasn't tempted to do so.

His world was Marika and he wanted no other. Because of her, he was more than he would have been otherwise.

Tallis opened his eyes to find Xanthus watching him, dragon arrogance and possessiveness in his stare as his body remained curled over Marika, his cock no doubt still inside her. He thought he'd won the unspoken masculine challenge between them, pleasured Marika beyond anything Tallis could do for her.

The dare for Tallis to prove otherwise radiated off Xanthus along with the waves of heat and pheromones. Tallis smiled, more a baring of teeth that anything else. He opened his mouth to tell Xanthus to get off Marika, then decided otherwise.

Let Xanthus feel her tremble with need. Let Xanthus know intimately just how thoroughly Marika craved another male.

Tallis crouched in front of her, his legs apart so his sac hung unhindered where she could press kisses to it, suck before taking his cock between her lips. His hands went to her hair, her face and she instinctively nuzzled into his palm.

"Open your eyes," he said, his heart softening at what he read in her face when she obeyed.

They'd have to allow her to rest for a while after he took her. She was Drui, more than human, but she was still young, no match for a mature Sjen or a dragon.

He didn't need to command her. She saw his need. Knew him as well as he knew her.

Soft lips brushed against his sac. Feminine moans sounded as she rubbed her tongue over the swollen globes of his testicles, sucked on them until his buttocks were clenching and his thigh muscles straining.

She was fucking herself on Xanthus' penis but Tallis didn't care. In the end it would be him, and not the dragon who rode her to completion.

Tallis tightened his fingers in her hair and she turned her attention to his cock. It was nearly unbearable to have her lips on his shaft, her tongue lashing him, tormenting the place where the spines lay flat.

He moaned, held himself steady as she moved on to tease the exposed head of his penis. He wanted Xanthus to witness his control of her, to *know* how thoroughly he and Marika were bonded.

She worshiped his cock as he'd taught her to do, was completely submissive, though he didn't doubt that after she rested for a while, she'd play her subtle games, challenge them to prove they could truly master her. He looked forward to it, counted on it.

"Take me in your mouth," Tallis said, prepared to punish her if she disobeyed.

But she didn't.

She took him. She sucked him.

And he fucked into her mouth, experienced the bliss of her lips and tongue and throat as they worked in concert to serve his pleasure.

He could easily have come. He *wanted* to come. Knew that by the time he pulled from her mouth and positioned himself behind her, he would be hard again.

Care for her kept him from giving in to his own desire. He'd proven his point to the dragon.

Tallis eased from Marika's mouth, his cock pulsing in violent protest when she whimpered at his abandonment.

Xanthus rolled away from her, his penis hard, wet, his face a mask of snarling masculine need.

Tallis covered her. Thrust hard and deep, and kept thrusting.

Words of love and desire tumbled from his lips and he was uncaring about having them overheard. She was his world, his heart, his soul. And while he and Xanthus might become lovers, it was only because of her, only because she was everything to both of them.

Tallis was beyond proving a point or answering a masculine challenge. All that mattered was being buried in her heat. All he cared about was being with her, reinforcing his claim to her and being as close to her as possible.

His movements grew frenzied. His control snapped. The spines on his penis descended, raking over her inner muscles and making her scream as orgasm slammed into her, pain and pleasure blending so she clamped down on his cock with viselike strength.

He came in violent shudders, had no more ability to stop the catlike sounds from escaping his throat than Xanthus had been able to conceal the dragon-shimmer, though Tallis knew the runes on his collar would keep Xanthus from guessing his true nature.

When his testicles were empty of semen, his sac no longer tight with the pressure to mate, Tallis collapsed to the side, taking Marika with him so she could rest. Through slitted eyes he saw Xanthus rise, felt approval, a deepening of the bond they were forming when the dragon padded over to the sunken tub.

Marika sighed and turned in Tallis' arms, making him hiss at the loss of her cunt. Her smile and soft laugh mollified him, as did the way she pressed a kiss to his lips, her eyes shining with happiness before she closed them again and nestled contentedly against him.

Tallis watched as Xanthus gathered towels and placed them near the tub, then went to a cabinet to retrieve a packaged bath sponge and liberated it, tossing it into the rapidly filling tub before opening a drawer and retrieving a tie for his hair.

The movements were confident, the dragon seemingly familiar with his surroundings and completely at ease with his nakedness. Tallis hardened when Xanthus shook out the white-blond hair and began to braid it, the position of his arms highlighting the muscled chest and taut abdomen, the jutting cock.

Tallis grew more aroused the longer he looked at Xanthus. He fought not to start purring in anticipation of battling with Xanthus for the dominant position, but lost when he felt Marika smile against his chest. With his erection pressed to her belly, she easily guessed the nature of his thoughts.

His rumbling purr deepened as he rubbed his cheek against her hair, an affectionate gesture that'd become instinctive when she'd melded his nature to a cat's. He knew the thought of seeing him with another man aroused her.

Xanthus' arms dropped to his sides when he'd finished braiding his hair. He turned and lifted an eyebrow in silent query before getting into the tub and turning off the water.

Tallis rose with Marika in his arms and padded over to the sunken tub, his testicles heavy and his cock on proud display. Lust roared through him, flickering along his nerve endings like dragon-fire when Xanthus' hand slipped beneath the water to his own hardened penis.

Their eyes met and held. In challenge and promise. In acknowledgement their sensual battle would begin once Marika was cared for.

"You've been on the *Sweet Surrender* before," Tallis said as he slid into the water with Marika and settled her between them.

"Yes, in the company of its previous owner and purely for business purposes." Xanthus laughed. "He lost at poker that night as well if I remember correctly."

Marika grinned, remembering Drake's Lair and gaming tables weighed down with treasure. "Do you play poker too?"

"Only with what I can afford to lose, and rarely with Pierce or Severn's cousin, Tielo, who co-owns Drake's Lair with Pierce."

Xanthus soaped the sponge. Tallis lathered his hands.

Marika felt the hard pulse of her heartbeat between her thighs when they began bathing her. She arched her back as they caressed her breasts.

She should be utterly exhausted, passed out from all the attention they'd given her and the sexual demands they'd made on her. Instead her body hummed with pleasure, her strength coming back and any soreness fading away with hot water and soapy caresses.

"I think I'll keep you both," she murmured, soaking in their beauty as well as the tender way they were caring for her. They were perfectly matched in physiques, lust-worthy by any measure. Especially hers.

Xanthus' hand moved downward to cup her mound. Her hips lifted with a sharp jerk when his palm pressed against her clit. "The outcome was never in doubt," he said.

Marika bit her bottom lip to keep from contradicting him. She cast a wary glance at Tallis, knowing how close she'd come to ending up with a mate of *his* choosing.

If the dragon guard had been hidden instead of casually positioned on a lounge chair just outside her apartment door... If she hadn't acted quickly to confine Tallis...

Tallis' eyes narrowed and his expression sent a shiver of erotic fear through her. "I haven't forgotten about punishing you for your actions," he said, his thoughts traveling the same path as hers, but reaching a different destination.

Marika lowered her eyelashes, felt her cheeks flush with the thought of having Xanthus witness whatever punishment Tallis intended. She moaned softly when Xanthus applied more pressure to her clit, its throbbing against his palm serving as a testament to how excited Tallis' threat made her.

"I'm glad Severn's mother showed up at Inner Magick today," she said, closing her eyes and giving herself over to sensation as they resumed bathing her.

The sponge glided down her spine. Xanthus' fingers slid into her channel. He said, "I never thought I'd be grateful to Severn's mother, but for once her arrogance has served a greater good."

"Will she go back home now the Chalice of Enos has been reclaimed?" Marika asked, grimacing at the prospect of having her show up at Inner Magick with her deadly bodyguards and at the thought of Sophie being saddled with the old dragon as a mother-in-law.

Xanthus chuckled. "I suspect she is already making plans to depart. Severn is her sole heir. He won't tolerate her presence if she doesn't fully and *graciously* accept Sophie as his choice of a mate. No doubt the thought of losing access to her future grandchildren is now playing heavily on her mind. She'll find it easier to avoid alienating him by returning to her home."

"Good," Marika said, wondering if Sophie knew yet about Severn's true nature, if she was even now in the dragon's realm.

Marika wished she could ask Xanthus. It would be so much easier if they could discuss things openly.

She and Xanthus weren't mated yet, but it didn't matter. Her heart and soul and body already belonged to him. Everything about him felt *right* to her. He would be her mate. She knew it as surely as she knew Tallis would always be with her.

Marika opened her eyes and turned her head slightly, pleaded silently with Tallis, asking him to release her from her promise to let him be the one to decide when they'd reveal themselves.

Tallis denied her with a subtle shake of his head, then turned his attention to Xanthus. "How is it you came to be working for Severn Damek?"

"I wanted to see the world and Severn offered me the opportunity to do so."

Marika worried her bottom lip. "You'll stay with him?"

Xanthus gave a casual shrug but his carefully neutral expression belied the gesture. "I have obligations to my family. At the moment I can't predict how they will play out."

His words flooded Marika with dread. She glanced at Tallis. His face was equally neutral.

"Obligations that will require you to live elsewhere?" Tallis asked.

"It wouldn't be my first choice. You and Marika are happy here?"

"This is home," Marika said, this time silently pleading with Xanthus to say he wouldn't ask her to leave it.

She rarely noticed the red and orange spikes of dragon energy any longer when it came to him, but her words made the signature colors deepen and swirl in fierce patterns. Xanthus leaned in and brushed his lips over hers, gentle despite the wild surge of his underlying emotions. "Your happiness is important to me. Never doubt it."

"I don't," she whispered, speaking the truth in her heart though fear for the future resided there too.

"What type of obligations hang over you with respect to your family?" Tallis asked.

"A distant relative with no heir. He's set a challenge in front of all the males he recognizes as part of his line. Whoever proves worthy enough will be named his heir."

Tension coiled in Marika's stomach, knotted into a hard tight ball. She could guess the nature of the challenge created by Xanthus' ancestor. Dragons valued treasure above all else. A Drui mate, even a Drui captive, might well make Xanthus an heir.

She glanced at Tallis. His face gave nothing away, but she knew he was considering what course to take, whether it was better to proceed and protect her by forming alliances, or to incapacitate Xanthus and take her away. The knot in her stomach tightened, grew harder as fear entwined with worry at what would happen if Xanthus and Tallis got into a *true* fight, not the sensual battle that Tallis' punishing her was sure to lead to.

It was cowardly not to want to think about the future. Marika knew that. But she believed they would find a way to overcome any obstacle to being together.

She trusted Xanthus. She trusted Tallis.

Nothing said was going to change the course of the night. Tomorrow morning she'd wake up a dragon's mate, claimed in every important way save for the final step of entering the dragon's realm.

Marika moved and turned so she was facing Tallis and Xanthus. One hand slid up Tallis' muscled thigh. The other did the same to Xanthus. She fondled their testicles before capturing their cocks, wanting to divert them from thoughts of the future by trapping them in the present.

Xanthus gave in easily. His hand joined hers, covering it and urging it up and down on his shaft. Tallis fought her, grabbed her wrist and held it prisoner though he didn't force her away from his penis.

He leaned forward, his growl a warm vibrating sound against her ear. "Your promise?"

She rubbed her cheek against his and gave him the only answer she could. "I'll keep it."

Growl turned into a soft purr. Tallis released her wrist, mimicked Xanthus by covering her hand with his, controlling the slide of it up and down his hardened penis.

Their cocks throbbed against her palms. Their expressions made lust dance in her belly like an erotic flame.

They were so incredibly gorgeous, so intoxicatingly sensual. They were masculine perfection. Protective, dominant, and yet capable of tenderness.

And they were hers.

If she'd had a cat form she would have purred in satisfaction. Her eyes went to the collar around Tallis' neck and she smiled in wicked amusement as she imagined fashioning a similar one for Xanthus to wear.

"What are you thinking?" Xanthus asked, drawing her attention to him.

Marika used her hands on their cocks to urge them closer to one another, so they sat side by side, their shoulders nearly touching. She knelt between their open thighs, getting as close to them as she could before leaning forward, kissing Xanthus because he didn't know her well enough yet to recognize the game she wanted to play.

She swallowed his moan. Deepened the kiss. Coaxed and seduced until he was trembling slightly, his tongue held hostage in her mouth as she sucked it to the same slow rhythm as she worked their cocks.

Only the need for air made her release him. She turned to Tallis. His eyes were slitted though not enough to hide the feral heat.

He let her play her game. Let her suck his tongue into her mouth as her hands tightened on their cocks, blending pain and pleasure as he'd taught her to do so the lust edged toward violence. But he exacted his own punishment, as did Xanthus.

Masculine fingers clamped down on her nipples. Sent spikes of white heat to her clit so she whimpered and rocked against their thighs, fought to remain in control of the play.

Marika relinquished Tallis' tongue and pulled away, rubbed her thumbs over their cock heads and felt the thrill of feminine power when their hips jerked and their breathing changed.

"I want to see you together," she said, stroking with her thumb, circling, finding the slits where their semen would erupt.

She arched her back when their fingers tightened on her nipples in reaction to her words and her teasing. Somehow she

123

managed to resist the urge to close her eyes and tilt her head back, baring her neck in a show of submission.

Before Tallis, she'd never guessed how thin the edge between pain and pleasure could be, or how much she'd enjoy riding it. Not all the time. Just as she didn't always want a dominant lover. But sometimes, when the mood was right, when playing games smoothed the way...

She gave them each another kiss, this one more aggressive than the first one. Knew they were tasting each other on her, growing more aroused by it.

Their bodies shifted subtly toward one another. "Let me see you together," she said, the lengths of their well-matched cocks allowing her to touch silky head to silky head.

They jerked back, the first instinct of dominant males. But she'd felt the hard throb of lust go through their shafts. She'd seen it flash across their faces. And now the desire smoldered in their eyes, looking for an outlet, a way to escape, like a fire ready to breach the barriers keeping it contained and tamed.

Marika lowered her lashes, already guessing what the catalyst for their loss of control would be. "Do you still think I should be punished?" she asked Tallis, her cunt lips filling with pulsing heat, parting further as she fantasized about Xanthus' watching Tallis discipline her, imagined the erotic violence contained in the scene stirring the dragon instinct to establish dominance in a fight for possession of a mate.

Little manipulator, Tallis thought, but the burning need that remained from the first touch of his cock to Xanthus' left him more than willing to be manipulated by her.

"Yes," he said, standing. Not surprised when her hand followed him, her fingers still locked around his cock.

Satisfaction fed his lust when both her eyes and Xanthus' immediately focused on the hard, thick length of his penis. It was time. Whatever complications existed because of Xanthus being dragon would be dealt with later. Tallis ached to know another man's touch again.

The first sexual encounter with Xanthus would start as a fight, a sensual battle for dominance. Xanthus' dragon nature would allow nothing else.

Tallis looked forward to, it, anticipated it. Arousal escaped the slit in his cock head at the thought of wrestling for supremacy while Marika looked on.

She was their prize, their possession. Their world and future.

Xanthus' heart would come to be equally ensnared by her, if it wasn't already. But until Tallis had a chance to form alliances with one or more of the dragon princes in order to ensure Marika remained in the human world, he had no intention of revealing her Drui heritage or his own Sjen nature. Whatever Xanthus' feelings, he was constricted by dragon laws and familial obligation. It would be a mistake to forget it.

"The suitcase is on the deck," Tallis said, circling her wrist and tugging gently.

He felt a primitive satisfaction when she released Xanthus' cock in favor of obeying the silent command to stand, when she blushed as she realized he intended to punish her on deck, where there was a chance someone might venture by the cove and witness it.

She reached for a towel but he stopped her. The warm night air would dry her, and until then, her slick skin would shine under the moon's light.

He loved fucking her under starry skies. Loved the way the breeze picked up her cries of pleasure and carried them into the night.

Xanthus stood, tension and anticipation radiating from him. He followed as Tallis guided Marika out of the stateroom.

The discarded pillowcase lay next to the suitcase, serving as a reminder of the indignity Tallis had suffered and the reason he would punish her. For a moment he considered using it to bind her wrists or blindfold her, then decided against it. He didn't know how the dragon would react at seeing her punished, didn't know how dangerous their fight for dominance would become before it was settled. He wanted her safe, and beyond that, he wanted her to witness what happened between Xanthus and him.

"Open the suitcase, Marika," Tallis said.

She knelt next to it, naked, the very picture of submission. Everything about her spoke to the primitive nature of man and beast alike, fired instincts of protectiveness as well as possessiveness.

It was all Tallis could do not to tumble her onto the deck and mount her. They'd been lovers for years and yet she still tested his control, made him hunger.

He spread his legs, only barely kept from groaning at the heavy feel of his testicles hanging beneath his cock. He crossed his arms over his chest, his posture that of a master over a slave.

The scent of her arousal tormented him. As did the sight of her slight trembling, the added color to her cheeks when the suitcase was opened to reveal the items he'd packed — the restraints there for Xanthus to see, the body oil and lubricant, the flogger.

Chapter Eleven

❧

Xanthus clenched his jaw to prevent any sound from escaping. He didn't know how much more he could stand before all pretense of being human was stripped away. He'd already endured more than he thought possible.

His fingers curled into fists at his sides when Marika picked up the flogger and demurely handed it to Tallis. She was so delicate, so beautiful. Xanthus wasn't sure he'd be able to tolerate having her skin reddened.

He crouched next to her, her scent enough to reassure him but he wanted to hear the words. "You want this?"

Marika shivered, keeping her eyes cast downward, her pose stirring his need to protect and possess even as the heat and scent surrounding her intensified, making him want to mount and mate her. She started to glance at Tallis, as if needing permission to speak, and the gesture inflamed Xanthus further.

"Answer me," he growled, "or Tallis won't be the only one punishing you tonight."

"Yes," she whispered, so soft, so submissive that Xanthus knew she was a master at this game, one who would keep him enslaved for a lifetime by offering him the chance to dominate her in this manner.

He stood, the hard ridges underneath his cock head throbbing as she rose gracefully to her feet and turned, placing her hands on the wall next to the stateroom door—inviting punishment.

For an instant his attention shifted to the other items in the suitcase. A pant escaped at the thought Marika tethered to the bed, held open and completely helpless.

The hidden spurs at this wrists tingled. But he knew he could resist the urge to rake them over her flesh if she was bound. He could draw out their mating. Make it last if she didn't touch him and if Tallis was left unconscious by the serum.

He met Tallis' gaze, understood that this was foreplay, not just between Marika and Tallis, but between Tallis and him. "How many lashes will you give her?"

"As many as it takes."

The answer made Xanthus' lips pull back in a snarl. "You are no longer the sole judge of that."

Tallis' eyes glinted a challenge in the moonlight. "That's yet to be determined between us."

Xanthus braced himself when Tallis' arm lifted. Dragon fire filled him when Marika moaned as Tallis struck her, a throaty sound that sent lust surging through Xanthus.

Tallis and Marika were beautiful together, their responses to one another fine-tuned, erotic to witness. Xanthus' hand went to his cock, working it with each stroke of the flogger.

Hunger built watching the play of Tallis' muscles, seeing the fine sheen of sweat coating his skin from his exertions, listening to Marika's whimpers of unrestrained submission. With each stroke, Xanthus' control slipped further until the magic concealing his true form threatened to burn away.

"Enough," Xanthus said, knowing he was close to shedding any pretense of being human.

"That's not for you to decide."

Tallis lifted his arm to continue his punishment. A growl was the only warning Xanthus gave, but it was enough. The flogger dropped to the deck as Tallis turned toward him with lithe, predatory grace, met his attack instead of retreating, their bodies straining as they wrestled and grappled, rolled and twisted.

At first there was no thought but the dragon's, no instinct other than to win the fight for dominance. But slowly Xanthus became aware of Tallis' scent, the feel of sweat and bath-slick skin against skin, the brush of a hardened penis or suede-soft testicles against his sides and back, his thighs. His cock.

The heat between them built, territorial battle giving way to a carnal one. Each twist, each brush of flesh against flesh feeding a hunger Xanthus had never experienced before meeting Tallis. It'd taken only a single glance at Tallis, only the knowledge that Tallis was Marika's lover to answer Xanthus' questions about his own sexuality.

Marika's presence made it more exciting. Feeling her eyes on them, knowing how much she liked seeing them together, how aroused she was at the prospect of witnessing one of them fuck the other made Xanthus ruthless, determined to be the victor.

His cock was slick, his testicles swollen and tight. His wrists tingled, the spurs ready to descend and rake across Tallis' chest in a primitive claiming.

Muscles strained. Skin touched and fingers and hands sought purchase.

With brutal accuracy Xanthus found Tallis' penis, gripped it, merging pain and pleasure as he forced Tallis onto knees and forearms. He could feel Tallis' cock throbbing against his palm, jerking as it grew wetter from having another man grip it.

"Yield," Xanthus growled. His relationship with Tallis was far from being defined but as his erection pressed against masculine buttocks and Tallis' no longer fought him, Xanthus wanted another man as he'd never wanted one before.

His hand tightened on Tallis' cock. Fire burned through his veins when Tallis' hips jerked and his thighs widened, yielding though he didn't voice his surrender.

Xanthus didn't care. He didn't insist on hearing the words because this carnal game would be played over and over again and he wouldn't always be the victor.

His gaze shifted from the muscular back and tanned skin in front of him to Marika. She was leaning against the stateroom wall, her hand between her thighs, delicate fingers slick as she toyed with her clit and thrust into her slit.

Lust was a roar in Xanthus' mind, a force that might have dropped him to his knees if he hadn't already been on them. The flogger rested at her feet, a reminder of the restraints he intended to use on her, the body oil and lubricant.

He forced his eyes away from her. The open suitcase was within arm's reach.

For a split second he considered having Marika bring the lubricant to him, put it on his cock and on the rosette of Tallis' anus. The tightening of his sac and the fire streaking up his spine warned him against it.

Another time he'd command her, enjoy making her a part of Tallis' subjugation. Not this time. Not when he'd be lucky if he managed to get all the way inside Tallis before he came.

Xanthus picked up the bottle of lubricant and thumbed it opened, coated his already arousal-slick cock before doing the same to Tallis' anus. His hand tightened on Tallis, as if to hold him still, to keep him from fighting the penetration, but there was no need. As soon as Xanthus pressed his cock head to Tallis' opening, Tallis rocked backward, moaned as he was breached.

An answering moan escaped Xanthus. Heat scorched through him and he closed his eyes, gave himself over completely to the darkly carnal taking of another man.

Though he was in the dominant position, it was hard to say who commanded and who answered the command. Lust ruled, burned away everything except the need to fuck as he slid deeper into Tallis.

Without conscious thought, Xanthus pressed closer, chest to back so as much skin as possible touched. With the first thrust he became a prisoner to sensation and frantic need.

His hand moved up and down on Tallis' penis. His moans blended with Tallis', became sharper, closer together until Tallis' cock spasmed, spewing seed and triggering Xanthus' own release. And in the mindless rush of orgasm, dragon spurs descended from his wrists to rake across Tallis' chest and abdomen.

They collapsed on the deck still joined, both of them lax though only Xanthus was conscious. He felt Marika's eyes on him. Heard the light panting sound of her breathing. Smelled her intoxicating scent.

Victory was sweet, arousing beyond measure. It coursed through him, a heady fire in his bloodstream that made his cock harden again.

"Tallis will want a rematch," she said in husky whisper. "He won't lose again. He'll fuck you until you pass out, just like he does me."

"He can try."

Dragon instinct urged Xanthus to lift his face to the sky and trumpet a song, to rake the spurs across Tallis for a second time before claiming Marika in a possessive mounting and doing the same to her. Reason and necessity — the desire to enjoy her while he had her to himself — dictated otherwise.

With a groan Xanthus pulled from Tallis' body. He felt no hint of the more powerful fey anywhere close, but he wouldn't leave Tallis on the deck, vulnerable to attack.

Dragon strength allowed him to lift Tallis into his arms and carry him to the couch in the stateroom. Feral satisfaction filled Xanthus at the sight of Tallis, his chest and belly coated with his own seed. It was the perfect erotic revenge, a punishment for all the times he'd woken alone in semen-wet sheets while Marika was in bed with Tallis.

Xanthus would have left Tallis where he lay, to wake with the evidence of spent passion on his skin. But Marika had other thoughts. And as she bathed Tallis with a sponge, Xanthus found himself mesmerized.

It was arousing to watch her glide the sponge over Tallis' golden skin and hardened muscles, to compare Tallis' masculine body to her delicate feminine form with its gentle curves. And in the moonlight coming through the stateroom windows her inner thighs glistened. Her nipples were hard tight points.

She liked to be watched. She liked to push her lovers. He saw it in the tiny tremors of her body, the slight smile as she used the stroke of the sponge to heighten his arousal with the same effectiveness as Tallis had used the flogger.

"Enough," Xanthus said, nearly purring when she immediately obeyed.

His hand circled her arm and she offered no resistance when he guided her away from Tallis and into the bathroom, then into the shower. A touch to the controls and heated water cascaded over them.

Xanthus spread his legs in silent command, nearly went to his knees when she began bathing him. Soft, soapy hands caressed his chest, toyed with his nipples and made his cock strain upward.

His abdomen quivered when she glided over the taut muscles. His testicles hung heavy beneath his throbbing cock.

A moan escaped when she cupped his sac, measuring its weight, sending white-heat through his penis. He was helpless to contain a second moan when the soap-slick fingers of her other hand slid up and down his cock as she leaned forward and suckled on a nipple.

Warring urges battled inside him. He wanted to order her onto her knees so he could fuck the mouth sending icy-hot shocks of lust to his penis. He wanted to turn her against the shower wall and take her as he'd taken Tallis, then pull out and plunge into her cunt, raking the spurs across her belly or breasts.

The faint shimmering blue of dragon color was evidence of how badly she affected his control. He struggled to remember his plan, his desire to spend time with her now that he finally had her to himself. She'd be unconscious for hours once the serum was injected.

Xanthus speared his hands through her hair, keeping her face to his chest as the dragon-color deepened, the magic holding him in human form wavering under the onslaught of his need to mate with her. He suffered the lash of her tongue. Thrust against her hands each time her teeth clamped down on his nipple.

Steam rose where the water struck his skin, his ability to contain the dragon fire lessening with each assault on his nipple. He might have given in to the overwhelming lust if she hadn't stopped her torment to whisper, "I want you inside me."

It was feminine command wrapped in a show of submission, a subtle challenge he couldn't allow to go unanswered. The hazy blue-magic faded as masculine pride and dragon will snapped his control back into place.

He used his fingers in her hair to tilt her head so his lips could cover hers in a punishing, dominating kiss. She whimpered and he swallowed the sound, fed on it. Her hands went to his chest in a show of supplication, though the fingers rubbing, tightening on his nipples warned him not to drop his guard when it came to her.

Thoughts of tying her to the bedframe sent savage hunger coiling around his cock. The image of the restraints, the memory of Tallis ordering her to open the suitcase, to hand him the flogger so he could punish her with it, gave Xanthus the strength to turn off the water and leave the shower stall.

She used a towel to dry him without being ordered to do it. Then dried herself, lingering in a way that told him Tallis liked to see her touching herself.

"Go get the restraints and the body oil," Xanthus said, dark pleasure coursing through him when erotic fear flickered in her eyes and she trembled even as the scent of her desire intensified at his command.

He was standing next to the couch when she returned, looking down at Tallis' sleep-softened features. Marika's hand reached, as if to stroke the hair back from Tallis' forehead, but Xanthus shackled her wrist, preventing contact for fear her touch might somehow wake Tallis from the serum-induced unconsciousness.

Pleading eyes met his. "Will you put him in bed with us, afterward?"

Tenderness flooded Xanthus, love and a burning desire to have her care for him as intensely as she cared for Tallis. He leaned down and kissed her, gave her softness and tenderness, moaned when her arms went around his neck and her naked skin pressed tightly to his in answer to his unspoken need to be close to her.

"I'll put him in bed with us," Xanthus said against her lips when the kiss ended, smiled as he added, "Despite having bested and mounted him, I accept him as my equal when it comes to you."

Marika's soft laugh was a sensuous stroke along Xanthus' spine and cock. He felt only anticipation as she repeated her earlier warning. "He won't lose again. He'll fuck you until you pass out, just like he does me."

Xanthus kissed her again, this time becoming aware of the items she held in her hands. The leather of the restraints trailed down his back. The plastic of the bottle was cool against his skin.

Her bare pussy was hot against his cock, a siren song tempting him to lift her, to impale her where they stood. He ached to be inside her, felt the phantom slide of the spurs from their sheaths.

There'd be no turning back if he entered her. She was sweet temptation, a soul-swallowing temptress who had already ensnared him.

Xanthus palmed her buttocks and found the will to resist her body's call to his by imagining her spread-eagled, held open and helpless for his pleasure. He wanted to bury his face between her thighs and greedily swallow her essence. He wanted to feel her sheath clamp hungrily on his tongue, to hear her screams as he sucked her tiny clit.

The roar of lust in his head and the relentless ache in his penis warned he didn't have time to play. He needed release. Needed the lava-hot rush of orgasm.

As if sensing his desperate need, Marika began sliding downward, to her knees. He stopped her with a harsh, "No."

Xanthus guided her to the bed and took the restraints and body oil from her hands, setting them on the nightstand — for later — though he knew there would only be a later if he came now, with her mouth sucking him as he worshiped her cunt with his lips and tongue.

He didn't stop her when she sat on the bed, easing backward, teasing him by spreading her legs to reveal her wet slit. He followed her on hands and knees, a low purr sounding when she retreated as he advanced, played the part of prey being stalked by a predator intent on devouring her completely.

Her games excited him. She might submit, but she'd never be thoroughly conquered.

Xanthus pounced when she reached the center of the huge bed. He had to fight the impulse to thrust into her channel. If he did, it would end too quickly and his victory over Tallis would be wasted.

He couldn't resist a kiss. A twining of tongues. A sensual battle that took place as fevered lips ate hungrily and throats swallowed the moans of pleasure.

"You've made my life nearly unbearable," he said when they parted for breath. "Every moment not given over to duty has been consumed with thoughts of you, with dreams of you."

"I've ached for you too," she said, making the lust in his belly twist and burn.

"You had Tallis to ease you."

She canted her hips, rubbed her flushed folds against his cock, coating it with her arousal. Her eyes were dark, heavy with need. "Is that what you think? What about your demonstration at Inner Magick before Severn's mother arrived? What was it you said?"

If he satisfied you completely then you wouldn't be wet for me.

Xanthus' cock jerked, urged him to seek out her hot opening. He closed his eyes to shore up his resistance.

She was wet. So, so wet despite what both he and Tallis had already done with her.

It occurred to him that he would probably never win an argument with her, not when a word, a touch, the sweet smell of her desire and the sight of her bare cunt left him completely defenseless. But he didn't care, didn't worry she would use her body as a weapon except in sensual battle.

"I should punish you," he whispered against her lips.

She laughed. "If you want."

Taunted, "Tallis likes to."

Dragon fire roared through Xanthus. He took her mouth again, kept it prisoner until it was his breath that fed her lungs, until she whimpered and softened in submission.

By the Great Shared Ancestor he wanted her. And yet somehow he forced himself away from her, knew satisfaction when she cried in protest, whispered, "No, please, I'll behave."

Xanthus rose to his knees, repositioned himself above her so he could explore her body as she did the same to him. He captured a nipple in his mouth, groaned as her tongue and teeth found his, as her lips suckled in the same rhythm as his did.

He lingered for as long as he dared, his cock leaving wet kisses each time it bobbed and touched his belly. She was so responsive, so uninhibited in giving and receiving pleasure. He knew he'd never tire of making love to her.

Xanthus moved lower, dipped his tongue into her bellybutton and felt Marika's trace the dragon rising from his hip. He panted, jerked as her hands glided over his buttocks before moving around to capture his cock and swollen sac. And then her mouth was there, licking, sucking, tormenting heated, hard flesh.

"Marika," he moaned, shuddering, burying his face between her thighs, uncaring any longer who was dominant and who was submissive as he ate her, pleasured her until she screamed, until she took him deep and swallowed his seed.

Afterward he tethered her loosely to the bedposts, her chest to the sheets. He straddled her, retrieved the body oil and dribbled it on her, laughed when she jerked and complained of its coolness.

"I'll warm you up," Xanthus all but purred, his hands smoothing over her supple, perfect skin, admiring sleek, feminine muscles and curves.

It surprised him how much pleasure he found in just touching her, in tending to her. Her moans were sweet music to his ears, filling him with joy and peace though he knew this was only a tender interlude, a chance to bond emotionally before he mounted her, mated her, claimed her completely with the raking of dragon spurs across her tender flesh.

He oiled his hands and slid them under her, cupping her breasts and finding hardened nipples. "That feels so good," she said, rubbing against him like a cat.

Chapter Twelve

ॐ

Xanthus leaned down, shuddered when his testicles encountered her buttocks. He pressed a kiss to her shoulder, fondled her breasts and lost himself in the heated scent of his mate.

There was no place on her body he didn't touch. His hands glided over every inch, lingered on any place that brought her pleasure.

"I love you this way," he said, one hand on her stomach, the other between her thighs, cupping her bare mound, rubbing, petting, telling her with his touch just how enthralled he was.

"I was afraid it would turn you off."

"Nothing about you could ever do that. There's nothing I wouldn't do with you if you desired it."

His hands slid around to her buttocks, lightly parted them. She jerked when his thumbs grazed her back entrance, then moved into the touch, fueling dark fantasies and making him ask, "Does Tallis take you there?"

"Yes," she whispered, the restraints taut as she canted her hips, offering not only a view of her tight rosette, but of her sultry intoxicating slit.

Xanthus brushed his thumbs over her anus again, thrilled at the way she quivered. "Have you fantasized about Tallis and I taking you at the same time? Do you want one of us filling your cunt while the other takes your ass?"

"Yes. Oh, yes."

Her breathless answer nearly stripped Xanthus of his control. He stroked the soft skin of her buttocks, promised, "The next time Tallis and I take you, we'll take you together."

Xanthus forced his hands to her hips, forced his thoughts away from the temptation of pressing his cock to her tight back entrance. He lifted her so there was no slack in her tethers. And then he slid his cock between her thighs so it stroked over her clit.

In a minute he would fuck her. But for now he let the dragon magic concealing the thick ridges beneath his cock head fade. He imagined taking her in his first form as he slid through her legs, rubbed himself against her tiny clit and bathed in her slick heat.

She was so sensual, so responsive. So quick to beg and plead.

He drew it out as long as he could. Refused to allow himself a release though he allowed her one.

She screamed his name. Whimpered it.

A dragon roar of satisfaction welled up in his chest. He pressed his lips to her shoulder to keep it from escaping, unsure enough of his control to be afraid he'd exhale fire if he gave in to the urge to announce his claiming of a mate.

"Please, make me yours," Marika said, rocking backward with what slack the tethers allowed, her words going straight to his heart and filling it with adoration.

He was too close. This time he wouldn't be able to keep from raking the spurs over her flesh.

Xanthus found the scar on her shoulder, the one he instinctively knew she'd gained from repeated mountings by her other mate. He took it between his teeth and slid into her slit.

With each thrust he fought to last just a little bit longer. With each thrust he reinforced his claim to her and bound himself more tightly to her.

He could share her, but he'd never let her be too far from him. When he was in the dragon realm, she would be with him. When he was among humans, she would be there.

A twinge of conscience made him remember their conversation in the tub and Marika calling this place home. Xanthus ruthlessly crushed the beginnings of guilt.

Tallis was strong, but he was still human. He couldn't protect Marika from the supernatural beings he was soon to discover existed, and Xanthus feared the fey would eventually seek a measure of revenge for his part in the dragons gaining possession of the Chalice of Enos.

Thoughts of the fey heightened Xanthus' need to not only mate with Marika, but to seal the bond by taking her to the dragon realm. White-heat rippled along his spine, a phantom flaring of the crest he had in his other form.

His skin glistened with sweat. As did hers. The air was laden with the scent of sex and satisfaction. Of two males who shared a female.

Xanthus resisted the urge to close his eyes and give in to primitive lust. To pound in and out of her as she was held captive by the tethers, symbolically enslaved to him.

The dragon wanted her like that. The man did too. And both would have her that way — but not this time.

In a heartbeat Xanthus realized he wanted her free. He wanted her face inches from his own, wanted to witness her pleasure and capture the moment when she knew the ecstasy of having the spurs pierce her, deepening the climax and sending her into oblivion.

He grunted, shuddered, nearly cried out in physical pain when he pulled out of her sheath, his torment echoed by her sob. It took only a moment to free wrists and ankles, to flip her onto her back.

They both moaned when his cock filled her and he settled heavily on her. "I'll never let you escape me," he said.

Her arms wrapped around his neck, tightened. "I don't want to escape."

He took her mouth. Her body. Gave her his heart, his soul, his dragon fire. Shouted in victory as they climaxed together and the serum making her a true dragon's mate pulsed into her through the hollow spurs.

Afterward he held her for long moments. Knew he purred and rumbled but he couldn't contain the sounds any more than he could contain his joy.

She'd tormented him by always remaining just out of reach. She'd repeatedly made him wake from dreams of her and sent him to the shower to take himself in hand.

Now, as he wallowed in the aftermath of claiming her, he knew he wouldn't change a thing about their courtship. He kissed her forehead, rubbed his cheek against hers, nuzzled her hair and ear. There was nothing dragons loved more than treasure, and the more difficult to obtain, the greater the pleasure.

She was his most priceless treasure and always would be. She was his greatest pleasure.

His attention shifted to Tallis. Tallis was a complication—an acceptable one—but a complication all the same.

Xanthus' cock stirred inside Marika's snug sheath at the memory of wrestling with Tallis and finally fucking him. He laughed softly as Marika's warning whispered through his mind. *Tallis will want a rematch. He won't lose. He'll fuck you until you pass out.*

Let him try. And try again.

Xanthus pressed a kiss to Marika's mouth then eased away from her. Tenderness and the need to care for her held his heart in its grip.

He padded to the bathroom, retrieved a fresh bath sponge and soaped it under warm water before grabbing a towel and returning to the bed.

Marika murmured in appreciation as he bathed her. He worshipped her with his eyes and hands, found as much satisfaction in caring for her as he did in dominating her.

For the first time since meeting her, he felt relaxed, almost completely sated. All that remained was to take her to the dragon realm.

If Tallis weren't involved he'd leave now for the portal. By the time Marika woke up she'd be in his cliff lair, naked and on a bed of glittering, smooth gems.

But Tallis was very much a part of equation. He couldn't be left behind unconscious. He *wouldn't* be left behind conscious. And beyond that, either conscious or unconscious, Xanthus couldn't carry both Tallis and Marika from the dragon-side gateway to his lair at the same time. His only viable option was to wait for the morning and take them to the portal house on some pretext, then usher them into the supernatural world.

Marika would handle the revelation well enough. He knew she was friends with other humans involved in various types of magic, and she'd be happy to learn Aislinn was half-elf, and that Sophie and Storm were also tied to supernatural beings.

The twinge of conscience returned, only this time he battled it with intellect rather than brute suppression. There was no reason to think if he succeeded in being named heir that he would need to remain in the dragon realm.

But you can't be sure, the voice of conscience insisted, further eroding Xanthus' contentment.

He set the sponge and towel aside then leaned forward to kiss Marika's flat, smooth belly. Images of watching her grow heavy with his child hardened his cock, though he had no intention of breeding her any time soon. He already had to share her with another. A child would be even more demanding of her time and attention than Tallis.

Xanthus smiled against her skin at the comparison of her other mate to a child. He gave her stomach another kiss before rising, intending to keep his promise to Marika and put Tallis in bed with them.

Shock surged through him like an electric current when he neared the couch and Tallis stood, free of the effects of the serum hours before Xanthus expected him to be. For an instant Xanthus wondered if it was possible Tallis was more than human, but shook the idea off with the realization that the primary purpose of the serum was to adapt a human's body for breeding with dragons. Such an adaptation wasn't required for Tallis.

Tallis traced his fingers over the places where the spurs had raked him. The skin was smooth, completely healed but the sight of him stroking the spots made Xanthus' cock bob and strain. "How much did you see?" he asked, glad that in the end he'd been face-to-face with Marika so there was little chance Tallis saw the spurs.

"Enough," Tallis said, his hand wrapping around his penis as his eyes traveled the length of Xanthus' body. "You won't make me pass out again."

It was a challenge, and yet the lack of heat in Tallis' voice and the way he stroked his own cock kept things from escalating as they had earlier, when he'd punished Marika and pushed Xanthus to the point of attacking him. Curiosity, aggression, lust, each of them swirled inside Xanthus along with the need to define his relationship with Tallis.

Xanthus circled his own cock, his hand mimicking Tallis. "Having you pass out again would only create more work for me. I've already had to carry you once and I promised Marika to place you in bed with us."

Tallis' gaze shifted to Marika then returned to Xanthus, his eyes dancing with carnal amusement. "Then let's not fight. She's not awake to witness it." He stepped forward, a lithe predator despite the lack of aggression.

Awkwardness made Xanthus stiffen. Heat crawled up his neck when surprised understanding flashed across Tallis' face.

"This is new to you? Being with another man?"

"It's not something I've experimented with."

Tallis crowded closer, his smile wicked. "Is that what I am to you, an experiment?"

"No," Xanthus managed, only barely suppressing a moan as their cocks touched. "My grandfather has a female mate as well as a male lover they both share. My father shares my mother with another male. I wasn't sure which example I would follow when I finally settled on a female of my own."

"Not your own," Tallis said, the growl in his voice a soft reminder rather than a true challenge. "Marika and I are inseparable."

"I have no desire to separate you."

"Good," Tallis said, wondering why he'd ever doubted Marika's choice in a second male for her bed. He was glad now that she'd eluded him, foiled his plan to take her away — not that he'd admit his error and offer her the flogger along with his back. The little minx already understood too well her power over him.

Xanthus was like no dragon Tallis had ever encountered or imagined encountering. He was a surprise, one Tallis intended to enjoy immensely.

Tallis couldn't stop himself from glancing at Marika. A purr rumbled in his chest at the peaceful expression on her face. It pleased him to see her content, sated. Even without the dragon serum, he suspected she would have been asleep by now, left exhausted by lovemaking.

His attention turned to Xanthus and he invaded the dragon's space with another step, with fingers curling around upper arms and lips only inches apart as the heat from their bodies and their scent mingled. Tallis could hear the thunder of Xanthus' heart, could feel muscles tensing underneath his hands.

Tallis waited for Xanthus to react, and in the wait, discovered how much he wanted an equal—not a male to be dominated or seduced—but a true partner, one who accepted his sexuality, gloried in it. A groan escaped when Xanthus closed the distance. Their lips and then their tongues meeting. Their breaths mingling as the beginnings of a bond formed.

It was ecstasy to Tallis, a pleasure that made his memories of other encounters—casual couplings before Marika—pale in comparison. Dragon fire poured into him, burning along his veins and making him more powerful.

Tallis ate at Xanthus' mouth, fed on magic and lust as their cocks rubbed, their testicles touching and the desire between them building, becoming an inferno. They were well matched in size, their bodies fitting perfectly—and Tallis wanted to claim every inch of Xanthus just as thoroughly as he'd done with Marika.

He slid to his knees, reveled in Xanthus' harsh breathing and hardened muscles, in the slight tremble that told him Xanthus knew what he intended and wouldn't say no. Marika might be the center of their worlds, but this was important too, more necessary than Tallis had let himself believe.

Perhaps in the darkest recesses of his mind he'd counted on being able to seduce whatever man Marika brought to their bed, convince him of how much pleasure could be had when two men made love to one another. It was a relief to touch and stroke masculine flesh without fear of remorse or repercussion, without worry about what the morning would bring.

Tallis captured Xanthus' penis, loved the way it throbbed against his palm, jerked as tiny tremors of need pulsed through it. It was hot steel covered in smooth, slick velvet, wet from Xanthus' semen and Marika's honeyed juices.

"You smell like her," Tallis said then rubbed his tongue over Xanthus' cock head. "You taste like her."

Xanthus moaned and hunched forward, dug his fingers in Tallis' hair. His desperate desire to be sucked making Tallis' penis ache for the same attention, viscerally reminding him of the scene he'd awakened to. Marika with Xanthus' cock in her mouth. Xanthus with his face pressed to her bare mound, pleasuring her with his lips and tongue.

Tallis took Xanthus deep, sucked the taste of Marika off him as Xanthus bucked and panted, became lost in an ecstasy that was different from what he found with Marika. There was no need for tenderness, no need for the gentle trappings of love between them. One day they would come to desire those things from one another, but for now it was raw, rough passion holding them enthralled and sealing the bond between them.

Experience gave Tallis an advantage. He took Xanthus to the edge of release repeatedly, only to retreat. He pushed Xanthus to the point where the dragon magic strained to conceal the ridges beneath the head of his penis.

A light sheen of sweat coated their skins, glistening in the moonlight streaming through the stateroom windows. Their breathing became harsh, the thunder of their hearts so loud it would be audible even to a human.

Dragon pheromones assaulted Tallis, nearly made him crazed with the desire to fuck. After their battle on the yacht deck, he would have been justified in driving Xanthus to his hands and knees, in demanding that he yield as Xanthus had demanded of him. But the remembered image of heat crawling up Xanthus' neck as he admitted to never having a male lover helped Tallis suppress the primitive desire to thoroughly dominate.

There'd be other days and nights to play games, to experiment and explore, to test the limits of trust and sensation. Tonight was about finding common ground, forming a connection that gave their relationship room to grow.

Tallis eased back. With his tongue he tormented the place where the dragon rings lay hidden by magic, his hand keeping Xanthus from either escaping or pressing deeper into his mouth. He was rewarded by moans, shudders, the tightening of Xanthus' fingers in his hair.

Xanthus' panting, the wild jerking of his hips told Tallis just how close Xanthus was to coming, how close he was to begging, though Tallis wouldn't insist—this time. And though Tallis would have liked to claim he was in complete control, it took incredible effort to release Xanthus' cock and stand, to keep from spewing his seed when his engorged penis rubbed Xanthus'.

Tallis retrieved the lubricant and coated his cock, then prepared Xanthus as Xanthus leaned over, gripped the back of the couch. "Push out when I push in," Tallis said when he placed the head of his penis against Xanthus' opening. It was the only help he was capable of giving as he fought the urge to enter in a single hard thrust.

Patience. The Sjen were capable of centuries of it and life with a young Drui had tested him, taught him the true value of it. Pleasure was worth waiting for, exquisite pleasure worth suffering for.

He pushed into Xanthus slowly, kept Xanthus from coming by taking his cock in hand, sweat beading as the sensation built and ecstasy remained just out of reach.

Xanthus' moans told him when to forge deeper. And when he was all the way in, Xanthus' rocking backward told him when to start fucking.

Tallis closed his eyes and gave in to desire. Let himself be taken by dragon heat and potent pheromones.

Power in the form of magic rushed into him. It was as hot and consuming as the lust burning through his veins and pulsing through his cock.

His moans joined Xanthus'. Blended perfectly as their cries and movements grew sharper, faster, until semen jetted through Xanthus' cock in pulsing waves, his release triggering Tallis'.

Afterward they showered then lay down on either side of Marika, their arms curling around her waist possessively and making her murmur and smile in her sleep. "I won't let you take her away from here," Tallis warned, his thoughts already moving forward, to forming alliances with Severn and perhaps the other dragon princes, Malik and Hakon.

Xanthus' eyes narrowed and his face tightened, his expression reminding Tallis that despite the intimacy they'd shared, and the tentative bond between them, Xanthus was his equal, a dominant male. "Her happiness is as important to me as it is to you, but I won't be parted from her."

Chapter Thirteen

ဢ

Marika woke to the sound of a boat's engine and the feel of masculine bodies tensing before rolling from the bed in a perfectly synchronized display of male protectiveness. She sat up and stretched, watched appreciatively as jeans were pulled over muscular thighs and semirigid cocks. But when both Xanthus and Tallis told her to stay before exiting the stateroom, her smile turned into a frown.

"Stay!" Marika grumbled, promptly leaving the bed and searching for something decent to wear.

The command struck her as very canine-oriented. Obviously a little bit of obedience had gone a $l - o - n - g$ way. Too far in fact. It'd gone to their heads and confused them.

Stay! Ha! She was more than happy to be submissive when it came to their sex life, but this was *real* life.

Stay, indeed.

She had to settle for a man's shirt. But with a little imagination, she figured whoever was rapidly approaching via a speedboat would guess she had a swimming suit on underneath the shirt. They were in Florida, after all.

Marika stepped out on deck and her amused aggravation crashed into true worry that something had happened to Sophie as Hakon, one of the dragon princes she knew by sight, approached the yacht.

Her hand found Tallis'. "Something's happened."

Tallis didn't offer a lie. He brushed his thumb over her knuckles. "Wait and see what news he brings before you imagine the worst."

Xanthus climbed down to where the small boat belonging to *Sweet Surrender* was anchored. But when he would have grabbed a line and tethered Hakon's boat, the prince shook his head. He cast only a cursory glance at Tallis and Marika before turning his full attention to Xanthus. "Your father arrived at Drake's Lair a short time ago. He's with Pierce now. Your grandmother was visiting a friend in this—here—one whose family has ties to those who would see the advantage of gaining favor with Otthilde.

"There's no proof of an attack other than the end result, but the timing speaks of vengeance over the loss of the chalice. Your grandmother's fading. In the short time it took for your grandfather to get her home, she could no longer rise from bed. Your grandfather thinks only the Aviah fruit can save her.

"Pierce believes he saw a cluster of mature plants when he was searching for treasure a few years back in the Amazon. I told your father I'd relay the news to you, and that perhaps you were in the midst of claiming a mate. There are volunteers willing to go with him to the Amazon, myself included. If we can find even one Aviah fruit..."

"This is my fault," Xanthus said, the raw pain in his voice lancing through Marika's heart. "You warned me there might be retaliation."

Marika's eyes sought Tallis', pleading with him to release her from her promise. She could help Xanthus' grandmother, she could draw out the fey poison that would soon leave her comatose.

If they were seeking the Aviah fruit then they thought Xanthus' grandmother had been attacked by someone using the crushed bodies of the rare insectlike Nara-fey. Alive, the Nara had stingers they used to incapacitate their prey, other fey or supernatural beings larger than they were, but still small, their victims usually no larger than the height of a hand. The toxin paralyzed, leaving prey alive, aware sometimes for days, as the Nara fed on both flesh and emotion.

"Please," Marika whispered, guessing at the thoughts racing through Tallis' mind.

The poison was quicker acting if the prey was fey, but a dragon could linger for months, perhaps years in a paralyzed state before the last reserves of their magic faded and the toxin killed them. Tallis would know that because Xanthus' grandmother was dragon she wasn't in immediate danger, not with Marika able to draw the poison away quickly. He'd assume there was time to form alliances to ensure they wouldn't be trapped in the dragon realm if they revealed themselves. But Marika couldn't bear the thought of Xanthus' grandmother lying helpless and frightened or Xanthus and his family suffering needlessly.

"Please," Marika whispered again.

Tallis wanted to deny her request. He wanted to further understand Xanthus' obligations to his family and why it was important to be named heir. He wanted a chance to speak with Severn or one of the other dragon princes if necessary in order to ensure Marika would be able to remain in the place she'd finally settled upon as home. But he wasn't immune to Xanthus' suffering or Marika's heartfelt desire to heal where she could.

It was Drui nature, the thing that had nearly led to their extinction at the hands of supernaturals and humans alike. It was Marika's nature, intensified by the bond she'd formed with Xanthus.

Trust. She'd trusted her instincts when she'd found him in an alleyway, afflicted by demon malaise, his spirit dying under the attack of dark magic. Even when she'd realized he wasn't the stray cat she'd thought she was tending, she hadn't pulled back and abandoned him to his fate. She'd continued to draw the evil away from him though it was risky, her preparations inadequate.

This thing with Xanthus is going to work out. Trust me, Tallis, she'd said through Storm's phone when she'd sent the Sidhes' wife to the apartment to retrieve him.

He glanced at Xanthus, now deep in conversation with Hakon about where they might find the Aviah fruit, how quickly they could get there and how best to divide the labor of searching. Their voices held confidence despite the unspoken truth they both knew, the Aviah fruit was rarer than the Nara. And even if the Aviah plant could be found, it bore fruit only once every five years.

Trust. Tallis could feel Marika's eyes on him, pleading with him, her silence a testament to her trust in him. She could break her promise and reveal her Drui heritage. He would still be bound to her, would still love her despite the anger and hurt her action would cause. They both knew that. They both knew *she* was his home and though he would prefer not to live in the dragon realm, in the end if she was trapped there, all that mattered to him was being with her.

Tallis turned his attention from the dragons. His eyes met Marika's. He stroked her cheek with the back of his hand. "You're sure?"

"Yes."

He leaned in and kissed her, a tender communion of spirit. "So be it."

Anguish and guilt ate at Xanthus. Despite Hakon's assertion that he wasn't to blame, he knew his grandmother lay stricken, dying because he'd not only kept Morgana from killing Sophie but because he'd been on the *Fortune's Child* to warn of Neryssa and Morgana's impending attack.

Pain clawed its way through his chest and up into his throat, choking him with unshed tears. The chances of saving his grandmother were slim. She was flower-fey, her nature as soft as a petal, her life-magic equally fragile, transitory.

A dragon with a vast hoard of ancient, magic-rich treasure might live years after being poisoned. A Sidhe, the most powerful of the fey would only linger for months before succumbing.

His stomach knotted. As it had from the first moment he'd met Marika, duty warred with desire. He wanted to take her and Tallis to the dragon realm and seal the bond between them, *needed* to know they were somewhere safe. But doing so would require time and explanation when every moment counted.

Despite his belief they would accept and adapt to the existence of the supernatural, he couldn't take them and abandon them, leaving them to cope with a revelation that drove some humans insane. Nor could he take them with him, not if he would be traveling through one of the portals linking places of this world together. And yet the thought of leaving them unguarded, where someone from Otthilde's court might act against them... How was he to choose between his grandmother and his mates?

Xanthus turned. His pain deepened at the sight of them kissing, oblivious to his suffering. His heart felt as though a fist was squeezing it mercilessly, wrenching away all the joy he'd felt since the Dragon's Cup was taken to Drake's Lair and he was free to come to Marika on the *Sweet Surrender*.

The embrace ended and they both looked at him. Tallis' face was taut, Marika's worried, anxious.

"There's no need to seek out the Aviah fruit," Tallis said. "Marika is Drui. If you'll promise to return her to this realm, we'll go with you to the dragon world and she will draw the Nara poison from your grandmother."

The words tilted Xanthus' reality on its axis. He was vaguely aware of Hakon saying, "If she's Drui, then you'll be made Kirill's heir for sure."

"You knew?" Xanthus asked Marika. "You've known since the day you walked into Aislinn's house and found me there guarding her?"

A slight nod. The tremble of Marika's bottom lip gave him her answer.

Xanthus fought the urge to breathe fire, to roar and rage as a way of deflecting the hurt at not being trusted. Keeping Tallis a secret was one thing but this...

The voice of conscience reminded him that he'd hidden his true nature from her, both dragon and sexual. One had been by choice, the other because of the covenants governing him.

Could he blame her for doing the same? Did he want to mar their newly formed bond with anger and misplaced hurt?

From what he'd witnessed during his time in this world, dating among ordinary humans was complicated. How could it be less when supernaturals from different cultures were drawn to one another?

May you have better control over Marika than I have over Sophie.

Severn's words flowed into Xanthus' thoughts, opening the gates so amusement and love could wash away the hurt and anger. Xanthus climbed the ladder to the deck, joining Tallis and Marika there.

"No more secrets between us," Xanthus said, brushing his lips against Marika's, then doing the same to Tallis, openly acknowledging them as both being his lovers in front of Hakon.

"There's something else you need to know," Marika whispered, her eyes asking him to wait until they were alone. "Let's tend to your grandmother first."

Xanthus nodded, but when he would have turned to address Hakon, Tallis' hand gripped his forearm, halting him with the hint of claws digging into his flesh. *Shapeshifter?* Xanthus wondered, no longer capable of being shocked.

Their eyes met and held. He found no answer in Tallis' hard gaze, only steely resolve.

"Regardless of what happens in the dragon realm, promise you'll return us to this world when we desire it," Tallis said.

The fist that had dropped away from Xanthus' heart tightened again, stirring his dragon nature to life, narrowing his focus to a single word. *Mine!*

Mine! It pulsed through him with every beat of his heart, sang in every cell and burned through his veins like fire. How could he promise to let them leave when duty might require him to stay? And yet how could he force them to stay if they desired to leave?

Trust. The very thing he'd agonized about only moments earlier had circled around to test him.

Once in the dragon realm there would be little chance of Marika and Tallis escaping. They would be subject to dragon law. And because they weren't dragon, they would be viewed as his treasure, his by right of possession even to the extent that any children Marika might bear would be belong to him by law — regardless of whether it was he or Tallis who fathered them.

Marika and Tallis were trusting him with their futures. He could do no less than be worthy of their trust and have faith that through compromise they could find a way to make their shared bond work. "I promise," he said, knowing it might make him appear weak to Hakon, but uncaring of it.

They delayed only long enough for Marika to get fully dressed. Then they left Hakon to return *Sweet Surrender* to the marina and get word to Xanthus' immediate family while they used the speedboat to get to the closest portal, one located on an island and capable of opening in any of the separate realms.

"Will the portal guardian require a payment?" Marika yelled, her hair whipping wildly in the speed-generated wind.

"Yes," Xanthus said.

The toll if they used the dragons' own gateway was set, though he'd pay a hefty price for taking Marika and Tallis through the first time. But it would cost them hours to get to that portal and he wouldn't risk his grandmother's life or delay and have her fear deepen as the poison spread, leaving her paralyzed.

Worry knotted his stomach. And as if sensing his distress, Marika and Tallis pushed through the wind to come to him.

Tallis' hand settled on Xanthus' shoulder, Marika's on his back and on his chest. Warmth flowed into Xanthus. Hope and love loosened the anxiety and fear. "Almost there," he said, slowing the boat and aiming for a narrow waterway.

Alligators lined the banks. Light gave way to darkness as they entered a forest of mangrove trees.

Dread filled Marika, a pervasive overwhelming sensation that made her short of breath even though she knew its source. The runes carved into the trees on either side of the water-path Xanthus was navigating were meant to turn the casual explorer back.

Burmese pythons, their thick bodies wrapped around limbs above the water, added to the threatening atmosphere. They were discarded pets drawn to the place by runes Marika recognized.

Xanthus turned onto another narrow waterway, then another before approaching two dark, ancient trees serving as sentinels. Their trunks were covered in symbols Marika knew were condensed magic, visible to her only because she was Drui.

The dread deepened the closer they got. She could almost hear whispering and suspected that had she been fully human, nightmare images would flood her subconscious.

Her heart thundered in her ears. Her hands tightened involuntarily on Xanthus.

Immense relief struck as soon as they passed through the tree-guarded opening, its impact as overwhelming as the dread had been. Marika fought to stay on her feet but finally gave up and sat down. "Are all the portals guarded like this one?"

"No," Xanthus said. "The portal defenses are unique to the guardian who controls it. This one doesn't belong to the dragons."

Marika rubbed her chest. "Who does it belong to?"

Xanthus shrugged. "Little is known about the guardian of this portal though as far as I know, he's held this gateway for long time."

The waterway they were on widened radically, then split into two separate paths, detouring around an island. Xanthus guided the speedboat to a dock while Marika probed the shadows beyond it, finally seeing a cabin that appeared to blend seamlessly into the trees surrounding it.

Tallis jumped easily onto the dock when they reached it and quickly secured the boat. Marika and Xanthus followed him.

"Hold on," Marika said, guessing it would cause a bigger delay if she waited until they entered the dragon realm to gather soil and place the oak seed in it in preparation for the healing of Xanthus' grandmother.

She knelt and scooped up a handful of rich dirt, placed it in a handkerchief Tallis held for her before taking a single seed from the locket she wore. Once the seed was buried in the dirt, Tallis used his claws to remove a thin strip of cloth from the handkerchief before closing it and tying it shut.

The cabin door opened just as Marika slipped the bundle of earth into her pocket. A man with a warrior's face and long, curling black hair emerged. He took only a few steps beyond the doorway before stopping, tanned muscular arms crossing over a bare chest.

Power radiated off him. It clung to him in midnight-blue while the tree shadows caressed him as if he were a part of them.

Marika had no clue what he was. She'd never encountered a being with a psychic signature like his.

His features tightened as they drew near, his focus sliding over Xanthus and Marika to settle on the collar around Tallis' neck. The gems braided into it flared to reveal the runes inscribed on them.

Eyes narrowed, midnight-blue irises that matched the guardian's aura became ruthlessly black. His arms fell away from his chest. His right hand balled into a fist, then opened to reveal a dark-sapphire globe. He held the globe out to Tallis and Tallis took it from him.

"You're enslaved?" he asked Tallis, his voice holding death.

Tallis reached up with his free hand and stroked the collar. "Not in any way I wouldn't willingly choose."

Silver sigils appeared in the globe's heart, forming and reforming until fading completely. The guardian nodded, took the globe from Tallis and closed his fingers around it as if compressing it until it could no longer be seen.

Midnight-blue eyes settled on Marika, his gaze sent a shiver up her spine. "It's not often a Drui seeks a portal." Masculine lips curved upward slightly as his attention shifted to Xanthus. "Especially in the company of a dragon and a shared mate." An elegant eyebrow lifted. "I assume that's the reason for your presence here, you wish to return to the dragon realm?"

"To the northern-most portal," Xanthus said. "What price do you require?"

The guardian's attention returned to Marika, lingered before moving on to Tallis. "A favor held in reserve for when I require it." His gaze moved back to Xanthus and the slight smile returned. "One that breaks no dragon law nor requires you to share your precious treasure."

Xanthus hesitated, opened his mouth to give his answer, then closed it and turned to Marika, silently including her in the decision.

Happiness flooded her heart at his gesture. "A favor held in reserve is fine with me," she said.

His eyes lifted to find Tallis'. Tallis nodded. "It's acceptable to me as well."

The guardian laughed in amusement, or perhaps in appreciation of Xanthus' undragonlike behavior. Either way, his voice held sensual, husky tones that stroked Marika's insides despite the fact she had no desire to have more than two lovers.

"We have an agreement?" the guardian asked.

"Yes," Xanthus said.

"It is done then," the guardian said. He turned toward the cabin door, touched his fingers to the silver and sapphire symbols embedded in the wood, his movements too quick, the pattern too complicated to remember.

When he was finished, he stepping away from the door. "You may enter."

Fear threatened to take hold of Marika. The portals often played a part in the scary tales told around Drui campfires. They were yawning mouths to swallow the unfortunate, terrifying, stomach-churning drops to a supernatural hell. They were pathways to imprisonment and the Drui who entered them were rarely seen again—*never* seen again in the case of her centuries-distant relatives.

Tallis took one of her hands. Xanthus took the other.

"I won't break my promise to you and Tallis," Xanthus said, stepping forward, pulling her into total darkness when she expected a living area with light streaming through the windows.

The door closed behind them and she felt...something. When it opened again, awe filled her.

Chapter Fourteen

ဆာ

Light flooded a stone-enclosed room instead of a wood-built one. And instead of swampland and waterways, snow-capped mountain ranges lifted toward the sky through a multitude of windows.

It defied explanation or logic. But then it would. It was a magic different than any Marika had experienced, stronger and more primitive than what remained in the world she called home. This place had been carved out by ancient, powerful dragons who'd fled a future where humans ruled by their sheer numbers, if not their technology.

Marika shivered as a cold breeze swept down from the snowy mountaintops. It surprised her. The few times when she'd let her fantasies extend to becoming Xanthus' mate, she'd imagined the dragon world to be one of heat, of prey-rich valleys and smooth ledges where sated beasts could sleep off a meal in sunshine.

Goose pimples rose on her arms. She was dressed for Florida not Alaska.

"I'm sorry," Xanthus said. "I didn't think to tell you to bring warmer clothing. I'm rarely in a human form when I'm here."

He released her hand. She thought he was going to become dragon, but instead he grasped the front of her shirt and tugged it out of the shorts she'd put on.

Marika gasped at the sight of the dark blue dragon with silver and scarlet streaks on her belly. It was a miniature of the one rising from Xanthus' hip.

The bond is sealed, he said, speaking into her mind and making her forget about the cold. Her heart raced. She'd heard it said that dragon mates could speak to each other telepathically.

Will we be able to speak like this when we return home?

Yes. Regardless of what form I'm in, as long as we are in the same realm, we are only a thought away from one another.

Marika's eyes sought Tallis'. His lips lifted in a silent snarl though his eyes hinted at dark amusement rather than real anger.

A glance downward revealed the same dragon rising from his hipbone. He touched it, flexed his fingers to reveal the claws he'd gained when she saved his life. *Remind me to leave my mark on your other mate the next time I tangle with him,* Tallis purred.

"You can try," Xanthus said, anticipation in his voice though it was replaced by concern as he added, "I need to take Marika to my grandparents' private lair. I can only carry one of you at a time. This place is considered neutral territory, but possession is at the root of most of our laws."

Xanthus' attention shifted to something behind them. Marika turned, felt the return of fear when she saw the shapes of dragons flying in the distance, soaring above a wide valley between two mountain ranges as if seeking prey.

"Take Marika now," Tallis said. "Don't concern yourself with fears for my safety. If the dragons come here seeking anything but transport, I'll amuse myself with them."

Tallis gave a playful growl as he took the panther's form, leaving Marika to gape. Whether fed by dragon magic because of the bond with Xanthus or because of their location, he was larger, heavier, even more lethal than he was in the human world.

"I believe Tallis can take care of himself," Xanthus said, some of the strain gone from his voice.

Marika didn't resist when he led her from the stone-crafted building with its paneless windows. But she did experience a moment of vertigo with the realization that the building and the ledge surrounding it formed a high dais only a winged creature could reach. To try to leave any other way would result in a fatal plunge to the ground far below.

The air around Xanthus shimmered blue with traces of silver and scarlet. Then he, too, was in his other form, magnificent just as Tallis was.

Xanthus' rumbling purr told her he'd caught her thoughts. *As long as I'm equal to Tallis in your mind, I am content,* he said, launching himself upward with an unfurling of wings. *Ready?*

Ready, Marika said, glad she'd skydived on a dare once and found she enjoyed it enough to do it several more times.

Xanthus swooped.

Despite trusting him completely, she still closed her eyes as he picked her up, curling her tightly to his chest before veering away from the dais. Cold air rushed over her, but the heat radiating from him kept her plenty warm.

Marika forced her eyes open, felt thrilled and awed at the same time. She could hear the flap of his wings, could see them in shadow far below.

In front of them were a multitude of valley pathways. She bent her neck to look behind them and even with an upside down view, she realized the dais with the stone building was in the center of a clearing, like the hub of a wheel with the valleys extending outward like spokes.

Marika started to form a question, but Xanthus' answer was already there in her mind. *The dais and clearing are the only neutral territory. Each valley belongs to a lair and is guarded by it. In the days before our fertility was tied to the wizard's cup and extinction became a threat, my kind would fight to the death for possession of the valleys, not just for access to the portal, but for the prey that roams the grasslands.*

And now?

We do not kill each other without great cause. Smaller, weaker lairs hold what is theirs through alliances and family members living close to one another. Access to a portal often involves payment of treasure to cross through another's territory.

Is that why you work for Severn? For an alliance and treasure?

In part, though in this realm it's Severn's mother who rules their ancestral lair.

Marika cringed, remembering the visit Severn's mother paid to Inner Magick. The comment she'd directed at Xanthus might have led to good things, but there was no dismissing the venom her words had held. If Severn's mother ruled here, then Marika doubted Xanthus' family benefited from it.

You are correct. She's powerful but these are lesser lands, sparse of game and colder than those at the southern end. My family's land is far removed from her influence. And beyond that, Severn has carved out his own kingdom among humans. With Sophie as his mate, there'll be even more reason to remain there.

Marika's stomach dropped as Xanthus dived, aiming for a narrow valley. *Is that what you wanted when you signed on with Severn? To stay in my world?*

Yes. Not all dragons can tolerate the limitations imposed by the human form and the rules that govern us in your world.

A growl vibrated along her back where it touched the smooth scales of his chest. Fire erupted in a fierce exhale, painting the air orange and red.

I found it frustrating myself when a certain female continued to elude me.

Marika laughed, allowing herself to enjoy the masculine display of aggravation before pressing forward with her questions. *And now?*

I would make my home wherever you desire.

She could hear the unspoken "but". Before she could ask him about it, he said, *This section of the valley is claimed by my distant relative, Kirill, the one seeking an heir.*

It was rugged land. Marika thought she saw herds of mountain goats or maybe big-horn sheep dotting the rocky mountain slopes. *Being named heir is important because of the portal or because of the prey?*

The portal. The lair held by my family is landlocked otherwise and not all of those taken as mates can stay in this world exclusively. My grandmother is one of them. She needs to return to your world periodically.

Xanthus banked to the left and trumpeted a call. In the distance he was answered and from his thoughts, Marika knew his grandmother was still alive but no longer able to speak or move.

Tension vibrated through Xanthus. The beat of his wings increased as he pushed himself harder.

Marika tried to block her thoughts, to keep her worry from spilling into his and increasing it. She was shocked at how quickly the Nara poison had reduced his grandmother to helplessness. A dragon—

Abruptly Marika realized his grandmother wasn't dragon, couldn't be if she needed to return to the human world periodically. She was most likely fey, of a type that didn't follow the Sidhe into the faerie realm.

Icy chills spiked through Marika's heart over what keeping her Drui heritage a secret might have meant. If they'd delayed, wanting to form alliances with Severn or one of the other dragon princes first before trusting Xanthus with the truth...

Marika shivered and closed her eyes, choosing to concentrate on what she would need to do instead of the tragedy that might have been. She mentally rehearsed so there'd be no wasted time, was only barely aware of Xanthus trumpeting again before banking right, then slowing and landing.

He shifted from dragon to human seamlessly, not putting her down until they were at his grandmother's side. She lay on a bed of yellow diamonds, tiny and humanlike, but not human. Her eyes were closed, her face aging, the soft gossamer clothing formed by petals drying and stiffening even as Marika watched. An orchid dying, the streaks of black in the fading pink and yellow aura confirming the presence of poison.

Are we too late? Xanthus asked, his pain becoming Marika's.

She took the bundle of soil from her pocket then sank to her knees and grasped his grandmother's hand. Whispered *I don't think so* into Xanthus' mind before giving herself over to the healing process.

The Nara-fey were rare, the poison they produced equally so, but Marika recognized it all the same. Be it instinct or cultural programming, because the Drui young traveled so extensively, by the time they finally settled down they held a great deal of knowledge they wouldn't otherwise have.

Silently she began the chant to draw away the poison, taking it into herself and changing it, pushing the altered magic through her palm to nourish the oak seed in its bed of earth. Roots emerged, followed by a shoot pushing through the loosely bundled handkerchief.

Marika lost all awareness of time and surroundings. There was only the chant, the blending of one repetition into the next without faltering so the poison was drawn out without being given the opportunity to renew its attack.

Xanthus' heart filled with love and gratitude as he watched life return to his grandmother. Brittle, hardened petals slowly softened, became nearly transparent again.

His attention shifted to the oak seedling in Marika's hand. He felt awe though he knew her talent could also instill terror. Centuries past the Drui ability to draw magic away and channel it elsewhere had nearly led to their extinction.

"I need to return to the portal for my other mate," Xanthus said, not wanting to leave Marika but knowing she'd be safe with his grandfather and his grandfather's male companion, Jakai.

They nodded, neither of them able to look away from the woman they loved. Xanthus stepped to the lair edge and launched himself into the sky.

He could feel Tallis' awareness of what was going on, his impatience as he stalked the portal chamber, almost willing a dragon to try to take him. A laugh welled up inside Xanthus, relief coupled with his sense of humor. *Are you so sure you could best one of my kind?*

Easily.

Should we test your claim when the three of us are in the privacy of my lair?

Tallis' purr slid through Xanthus' body to curl around his cock. *If you wish. But perhaps you should keep your promise to Marika first.*

Moonlit images assaulted Xanthus. Moments captured in Tallis' memory as well as his own.

Marika tethered to the bed with him brushing his thumbs over her anus, saying, "Have you fantasized about Tallis and I taking you at the same time? Do you want one of us filling your cunt while the other takes your ass?"

Of her breathless answer. "Yes. Oh, yes."

And his promise. "The next time Tallis and I take you, we'll take you together."

Fantasy followed memory. Tallis' desires blending with his own, a carnal dance slipped into naturally, the two of them in human form once again, making love to Marika before turning their attention to one another.

The portal came into view, and with it the pacing panther. The gold of Tallis' fur glinted in the sunshine. *It'll be easier to carry you in your human form.*

Tallis answered by shifting. Within minutes Xanthus swooped in and picked him up.

In the dragon realm Tallis couldn't hide what he was. Despite the human and cat forms, Xanthus knew Tallis was a shapeshifter only in the sense he himself was. Similar, but different to the Were creatures who still called the human world home.

It was a subtle difference, one difficult for Xanthus to clearly define even to himself though he tried. The Weres were dual-natured, a blending of beast and man. While dragons...

Dragons were the first supernatural beings to emerge from the latent magic of the world the humans now claimed. They went for centuries, perhaps millennium in their first form. Many of the truly ancient had never taken a human form and many more might not have elected to do so if the wizard Enos hadn't created his cursed cup, changing dragon culture so human women became even more desirable as mates. His kind might change shape and look human, but it was a façade. Their nature remained wholly dragon.

Xanthus knew little about the Sjen, but he could feel Tallis drawing on dragon magic, being made stronger not just by the bond with Marika but the bond the two of them shared. It might have alarmed Xanthus except for having grown up seeing the relationship his grandfather shared with Jakai.

Unlike Xanthus' grandmother, Jakai was fire-fey. He had no need to return to the human world to restore his magic, not when he shared a bed and life with a dragon.

How did you come to be with Marika? Xanthus asked, thinking perhaps the answer would help him better understand what a Sjen was.

Once again Tallis' memories played out in Xanthus' mind, this time of Tallis' past with Marika. He saw her mistaken belief Tallis was an alley cat, her courage to continue trying to save Tallis' life even though he'd been attacked by black magic, his spirit under demon assault. Xanthus saw how Marika's actions bound Tallis to her, changed him, blending cat and man and guardian into something no longer completely Sjen. He saw too how much stronger Tallis was because Marika had chosen a dragon for a mate.

It didn't bother Xanthus. In fact, it pleased him.

He'd worried about Marika taking a human male for a mate, someone who was powerless to protect her against a supernatural threat. And though he'd resigned himself to accepting her choice, it was a relief to know he didn't have to fear for her safety. Tallis was more than capable of protecting her.

With a thought Xanthus turned his attention to Marika. The chanting that had filled her mind was no longer present. Instead she was talking to his grandmother, running a healer's hands over fey flesh to make sure no Nara poison remained.

Relief filled Xanthus. Joy and love such as he'd never known.

Do you wish to be taken to my grandparents' lair? Xanthus asked Tallis. *Or do you want to be taken to mine?*

Tallis hesitated only a moment before answering, sending sultry heat along with his words. *Yours. There'll be time later for introductions.*

Xanthus deposited Tallis on a rocky ledge a short time later. He circled only long enough to witness Tallis changing into a panther's form and padding into the depths of the lair before he turned and headed back in the direction he'd come from.

The sound of leathery wingbeats reached him, followed by the dragon song of his distant relative. Xanthus' own wingbeats faltered, then sped up as it became clear Kirill was heading for his grandparents' lair.

They arrived almost at the same time, neither of them shedding the dragon form. Xanthus spared only a glance toward Marika but couldn't see her. His grandfather had taken his first form to better guard both his mate and Xanthus'. Jakai stood next to him, ready to add his fire to the battle should there be one.

Chapter Fifteen

ಶಾ

Time slowed, the moments crawling past. It was always a careful dance when a dragon who didn't share close family ties or friendship stepped into another's private lair, especially a lair holding a non-dragon mate.

Kirill's attention shifted to the unseen females. His nostrils flared. The yellow of his irises spiked with orange an instant before there was the shimmer of magic being forced into human shape.

The tension in the lair subsided immediately. Xanthus easily took his second form, smiled privately with the realization that since joining Severn in the human realm, he no longer preferred one form to the other, but saw the benefits of each.

His grandfather changed forms, too, asked, "What brings you here, Kirill?"

"News of the attack on your fey mate. When Xanthus passed through my lands I thought he returned not only with a mate, but with the Aviah fruit. Such a feat would perhaps allow me to see some advantage to the fey blood that's found its way into my bloodline and name Xanthus my heir as a result. But now I find he's accomplished something even more worthy. He brought a Drui here." The orange in Kirill's irises bled further into the yellow as he turned his attention to Xanthus. "Your mate? Or a treasure you might part with in order to be named heir?"

"My mate."

"I would like to see this mate for myself."

Xanthus stiffened, fighting against natural inclinations to guard and hoard. Until Kirill's announcement that he intended to name an heir so he could leave his lands and hoard protected while he traveled in the human world, he had been a solitary creature. In all the important ways, he was a stranger regardless of his blood-tie.

Possessiveness burned through Xanthus' veins along with the heated desire of a newly mated dragon to return to his lair with his female and remain there, coupling with her constantly. His heart was a battleground between duty and need. But when had it ever been otherwise when Marika was involved? Reluctantly Xanthus nodded.

His grandfather and Jakai moved aside just enough to reveal Marika. Love flared at the sight of her, a white-hot emotion that intensified when she smiled at him, her eyes shining with her own feelings.

Marika stood, tears of happiness clogging her throat. When she thought of how differently things could have turned out if she'd said no to Xanthus because he was a dragon... If she'd left Florida and returned only after taking a second mate...

If that had happened, Xanthus purred, *then you would have ended up with three men in your bed. Your fate as a dragon's mate was sealed the moment you walked into Aislinn's home.*

Laughter settled in Marika's chest. Dragons! They were TROUBLE. In all caps.

She stepped between Xanthus' grandfather and Jakai and wasn't a bit surprised when Xanthus shackled her wrist and pulled her into his arms. She settled against his chest, her smile widening at the low purr vibrating along her back.

Marika doubted Xanthus was even aware of the sound, though it made need pool in her belly, a desire that intensified when his hand glided downward, stroking over her abdomen and the magic-inscribed tattoo that'd appeared there when she entered this realm. His fingers found the hem of her shirt, lifted it just enough to reveal the dragon, its image matching the one he wore in his human shape and identical to the one he became in this world.

"My mate," Xanthus said. "Marika."

"And the male you carried to your lair?" Kirill asked.

"Also mine."

The orange in Kirill's irises shrank backward, as if the thought of Xanthus with another male somehow offset the value of having taken a Drui mate. His reaction didn't surprise Marika, but the change in his eye color did. She knew there were fey whose color altered depending on their mood, but she'd never heard of a dragon's eyes revealing emotion or thought in such a way.

It's not common among us, Xanthus said. *Little is known about Kirill, though my mother once told me she'd heard her grandparents speak of him once and say he'd tried to steal from a powerful sorcerer long ago, before the dragons fashioned this realm, and been cursed in the process.*

Marika studied Kirill more closely. It startled her when she realized she couldn't see the signature energy patterns of a dragon surrounding him. A quick glance at Xanthus and his grandfather revealed the same was true of them, making her think perhaps the reason she could see it in her world was because their magic sparked and flared in a place that was magic-poor because of the exodus of the oldest and most powerful of the supernaturals.

If Kirill was indeed cursed, she wouldn't know it unless she touched him. And even if he were cursed, there was no guarantee she could draw the dark magic away from him.

"You will remain here with your mates?" Kirill asked Xanthus.

Xanthus tensed against her back. She could sense the struggle inside him, his desire to be with her and Tallis warring with the duty he felt toward his family.

"For now I am here," Xanthus carefully answered, silently adding, *I have not forgotten my promise to you and Tallis.*

Kirill's irises flashed to red. *In alarm*, Marika thought. And his next words seemed to confirm it. "A Drui is too great a treasure to risk in the human world."

Xanthus' arms tightened around Marika. "Where my mates and I choose to settle is between us."

The red of Kirill's irises darkened, scarlet becoming carmine. "Agree to keep her in the dragon's realm and I'll name you heir."

There was no hesitation in Xanthus, not even a flicker of temptation in his thoughts. "No," he said.

Carmine irises darkened almost to black. Kirill glanced quickly in the direction of Xanthus' fey grandmother. "If not you as heir, then I'll name Ormetri."

Marika felt the alarm the name caused. But before she could ask Xanthus who Ormetri was, the answer was already being provided. *He is another of Kirill's distant relatives, one who hates the fey and would never allow my grandmother to pass to and from the portal.*

Xanthus' grandfather stepped forward and said, "Save your threats and your promises, Kirill. Keeping Marika here against her will would be poor payment for saving the life of my mate. I will continue to pay tribute for passage through your lands until such time as Ormetri takes over and denies access, but I won't allow you to force Xanthus into making his mate a prisoner."

"By your choice," Kirill said, his attention shifting to Xanthus'. "It is yours as well?"

Wait, Marika said, stopping Xanthus before he could speak. She reached out mentally for Tallis.

Words tangled inside her, a confused conflict of needs and desires. Home was Florida. Inner Magick. Aislinn, Storm and Sophie. Sandy beaches and the sound of gulls. But home was also Xanthus and Tallis. With them she could be happy anywhere.

I don't want Xanthus' family to suffer because of the promise he made to us, Marika said, trying to block her thoughts from Xanthus but unsure whether she was succeeding or not.

You're my world, Tallis reminded her, his voice a warm stroke across her soul. *If you choose to stay here, then I will accept that choice.*

Marika studied Kirill again, played the conversation since his arrival over in her mind, let intuition guide her. This time she took down the mental barrier she'd erected before speaking. *If he's truly the victim of a sorcerer's curse, then perhaps he is thinking that one day he might trust me to cure him.*

Behind her Xanthus stilled completely. Tallis said, *Healing him would require you to lay your hands on him and touch the magic that's his life-blood. He knows the Drui are capable of draining away all power just as easily as they're capable of drawing out only the dark taint left by a spell. If you are right, then he might one day release Xanthus from a pledge to keep you here.*

But if I am wrong…

I won't have you unhappy, Xanthus said. *I will tell Kirill my answer is no.*

Marika covered Xanthus' arms with hers, entwined her fingers with his. "I will agree to stay in this realm if you'll make Xanthus your heir," she said.

Black irises lightened, passed through carmine and scarlet to become fully orange. "Agreed. If you'll accompany me —"

"No," Xanthus interrupted. "It is enough for now that my mate has promised to stay in the dragon realm. We can work out the details of our agreement and seal them with a blood-oath later."

Orange gave way to yellow and amusement. "Forgive me. With all that's transpired, I forgot you'd only just returned home with new mates. Come to my lair when you are ready and we will finalize the details naming you heir and granting you rights to my land as well as spelling out your responsibilities to it and to me."

He bowed slightly, an Old World gesture making Marika optimistic she'd come to like Kirill, and he'd come to trust her enough to allow her to try to heal him—if her guess proved correct. And if she was wrong, she could always fall back on the lure of treasure.

In her Drui wanderlust, she'd learned about more than healing. She'd listened to countless tales of lost riches and buried ruins. Searching for them wasn't something she and Tallis had ever cared to pursue, but being mated to a dragon might change things.

Xanthus' laughter rumbled through her, a husky purr in her mind. *I'll hear these tales. Later. Much later. After I've had a chance to thoroughly investigate my recently claimed treasure.*

His arms pulled away from hers, his hands sliding over her belly before he picked her up. To Kirill he said, "I will seek you out after my mates have settled."

Xanthus didn't wait for a reply. Magic shimmered around them, pouring into Marika like a sensual charge of electricity.

How he managed to shift and launch himself into flight, Marika didn't know. But she was once again in the air, the valley floor far below.

Anticipation mounted with each stroke of dark blue wings, built as they soared even higher before banking sharply and entering a narrow gorge. Their abrupt appearance scattered a herd of bighorn sheep, and then she saw the opening in the cliffs.

Marika felt a moment's vertigo at the sheer drop below the ledge Tallis was padding along in the panther's form. He stepped back from the edge, allowing Xanthus space to land, changed to a human form even as Xanthus was doing the same with Marika in his arms.

"I thought the two of you were never going to get here," Tallis said, closing the distance so his naked chest touched Xanthus' arm and Marika.

Like Tallis, Xanthus could shift with or without clothes. And like Tallis, this time he was naked, his body heat and Xanthus' enclosing her in an intimate cocoon.

Desire poured into Marika. Need swamped her so she was barely aware of the glittering jewels in the lair and the wealth they represented in the human world.

"No clothing allowed unless we give you permission," Xanthus said, setting her on her feet, nuzzling her hair as his hands went to her shorts, unbuttoning and unzipping, pushing them downward along with her panties.

Tallis claimed her mouth. Practiced fingers opened her shirt and unclasped her bra, slid them off her shoulders to fall to the floor.

Marika moaned when he kissed downward to her bare cunt, lapping at her wet slit and clit as he removed her shoes. She arched her back when Xanthus' hands cupped her breasts and his mouth found the mating scar on her shoulder.

You promised, she whispered in their minds, remembering Xanthus' thumbs stroking over her back entrance, telling her that he and Tallis would take her at the same time the next time they coupled.

So I did, Xanthus said, and she felt the effort it cost him to step away from her, his unwillingness to lose all contact with her as he took her hand.

Tallis rose to his feet. He claimed her lips in a feral kiss that tasted of her own arousal before mimicking Xanthus' actions, stepping back and taking her hand.

They led her to the bed of glittering gems. Diamonds. Rubies. Emeralds. Opals. Others she didn't have time to identify. She couldn't imagine they'd be comfortable, and yet when Xanthus and Tallis sat, tugging her down to sit with them, she found the stones were smooth, strangely warm, their mass conforming like a beanbag chair.

A treasure chest caught her eye, the artistry on its surface magnificent. Delicate images of dragons and fey were engraved on its surface.

Marika leaned closer to study it, realized the fey entities were fire and flower fairies, like Xanthus' grandmother and Jakai. Intuition made her ask, "Did you make this?"

"Yes."

She lightly traced the carved images. "It's beautiful. Exquisite."

"It's custom among dragon males to set aside gifts for a new mate. The chest and its contents are for you." There was just the barest hint of vulnerability, felt rather than heard before Xanthus masked it with humor. "You may share with Tallis. Or not."

Love made Marika's heart swell. Xanthus was such a surprise, so different than she'd imagined a dragon mate would be. Oh, she didn't doubt he could huff and puff and burn the house down if he didn't get his own way. And she already knew he was possessive and dominating. But instead of a man who didn't know the meaning of carefree because he was weighed down by all the treasure he felt compelled to guard, Xanthus was bound by honor and duty.

She could live with that. Why she'd even bothered fighting the Drui instinct when it came to choosing and claiming a mate, she didn't know. In fact, she couldn't imagine a more perfect match for her and Tallis.

True, Tallis purred into her thoughts, his satisfaction rumbling through her and making her labia swell and part.

Marika put her hand on Xanthus' chest and pushed so he sprawled backward on the bed of gems, a dragon lying on his hoard. She crawled on top of him, made him moan when her hand circled his hard cock, fingers gliding over the thick rings beneath the tip that he no longer had to hide from her.

"I think we've already determined that I like to share with Tallis," she said, guiding him to her slick entrance and taking him inside her, the muscles of her sheath rippling and clinging, spasming in ecstasy.

Her lips touched Xanthus'. Their tongues met, tangled in a sharing that transcended the physical, encompassed so much more. He breathed his dragon fire into her, but its heat was nothing compared to their combined lust, a merging of three into one.

Xanthus' hands slid down her back to her buttocks, parted them in a carnal offering to Tallis. *And I've found I like sharing my treasure with Tallis as well,* he said, moaning into her mouth when Tallis heat and scent was added to theirs.

Marika whimpered when Tallis' arousal-slick cock head pressed to her back entrance. *Yes,* she said, *oh yes.* And Tallis pushed into her, slowly worked his way deeper and deeper, his cock rubbing against Xanthus', separated by only a thin barrier, the three of them joined intimately, permanently, their pleasure blending, their futures merging in a Drui claiming.

ℰℓso by Jory Strong

📖

Carnival Tarot 1: Sarael's Reading
Carnival Tarot 2: Kiziah's Reading
Carnival Tarot 3: Dakotah's Reading
Crime Tells 1: Lyric's Cop
Crime Tells 2: Cady's Cowboy
Crime Tells 3: Calista's Men
Death's Courtship
Ellora's Cavemen: Dreams of the Oasis I (*anthology*)
Ellora's Cavemen: Seasons of Seduction I (*anthology*)
Ellora's Cavemen: Seasons of Seduction IV (*anthology*)
Elven Surrender
Fallon Mates 1: Binding Krista
Fallon Mates 2: Zeraac's Miracle
Fallon Mates 3: Roping Savannah
Familiar Pleasures
Spirit Flight
Spirits Shared
Supernatural Bonds 1: Trace's Psychic
Supernatural Bonds 2: Storm's Faeries
Supernatural Bonds 3: Sophie's Dragon
The Angelini 1: Skye's Trail
The Angelini 2: Syndelle's Possession
The Angelini 3: Mystic's Run
Two Spirits

About the Author

ဆာ

Jory has been writing since childhood and has never outgrown being a daydreamer. When she's not hunched over her computer, lost in the muse and conjuring up new heroes and heroines, she can usually be found reading, riding her horses, or hiking with her dogs.

Jory welcomes comments from readers. You can find her website and email address on her author bio page at www.ellorascave.com.

Tell Us What You Think

We appreciate hearing reader opinions about our books. You can email us at Comments@EllorasCave.com.

Why an electronic book?

We live in the Information Age—an exciting time in the history of human civilization, in which technology rules supreme and continues to progress in leaps and bounds every minute of every day. For a multitude of reasons, more and more avid literary fans are opting to purchase e-books instead of paper books. The question from those not yet initiated into the world of electronic reading is simply: *Why?*

1. *Price.* An electronic title at Ellora's Cave Publishing and Cerridwen Press runs anywhere from 40% to 75% less than the cover price of the exact same title in paperback format. Why? Basic mathematics and cost. It is less expensive to publish an e-book (no paper and printing, no warehousing and shipping) than it is to publish a paperback, so the savings are passed along to the consumer.

2. *Space.* Running out of room in your house for your books? That is one worry you will never have with electronic books. For a low one-time cost, you can purchase a handheld device specifically designed for e-reading. Many e-readers have large, convenient screens for viewing. Better yet, hundreds of titles can be stored within your new library—on a single microchip. There are a variety of e-readers from different manufacturers. You can also read e-books on your PC or laptop computer. (Please note that Ellora's Cave does not endorse any specific brands.

You can check our websites at www.ellorascave.com or www.cerridwenpress.com for information we make available to new consumers.)

3. *Mobility.* Because your new e-library consists of only a microchip within a small, easily transportable e-reader, your entire cache of books can be taken with you wherever you go.

4. ***Personal Viewing Preferences.*** Are the words you are currently reading too small? Too large? Too... ANNOYING? Paperback books cannot be modified according to personal preferences, but e-books can.

5. ***Instant Gratification.*** Is it the middle of the night and all the bookstores near you are closed? Are you tired of waiting days, sometimes weeks, for bookstores to ship the novels you bought? Ellora's Cave Publishing sells instantaneous downloads twenty-four hours a day, seven days a week, every day of the year. Our webstore is never closed. Our e-book delivery system is 100% automated, meaning your order is filled as soon as you pay for it.

Those are a few of the top reasons why electronic books are replacing paperbacks for many avid readers.

As always, Ellora's Cave and Cerridwen Press welcome your questions and comments. We invite you to email us at Comments@ellorascave.com or write to us directly at Ellora's Cave Publishing Inc., 1056 Home Avenue, Akron, OH 44310-3502.

COMING TO A BOOKSTORE NEAR YOU!

ELLORA'S CAVE

Bestselling Authors Tour

UPDATES AVAILABLE AT

WWW.ELLORASCAVE.COM

erridwen, the Celtic Goddess of wisdom, was the muse who brought inspiration to story-tellers and those in the creative arts. Cerridwen Press encompasses the best and most innovative stories in all genres of today's fiction. Visit our site and discover the newest titles by talented authors who still get inspired - much like the ancient storytellers did, once upon a time.

CERRIDWEN PRESS
WWW.CERRIDWENPRESS.COM

*Discover for yourself why readers can't get enough
of the multiple award-winning publisher*

Ellora's Cave.

*Whether you prefer e-books or paperbacks,
be sure to visit EC on the web at
www.ellorascave.com*

*for an erotic reading experience that will leave you
breathless.*

1055998R0

Printed in Great Britain by
Amazon.co.uk, Ltd.,
Marston Gate.